"I have the right to an attorney!" Andy Uchello exclaimed.

Andy gripped her foam cup tighter and glanced around the airport security office. For the past hour, she'd been sitting in this stark room, trying to explain why she'd picked up another person's briefcase at baggage claim.

"You're going to need a damn good one," Victor Mondragon said in a tone made all the more disturbing because he'd whispered right into her ear.

"I demand to use the phone!" Andy said.

"Fine." Victor watched her rise. He liked women, liked all of them: tall and willowy, curvaceous or athletic, blond, brunette or redhead. And he couldn't help but be aware of this one.

But she was possibly dangerous. Yes, something was up. And Victor would bet his badge that Andy Uchello was in it up to her pretty little neck.

Dear Reader,

Be prepared to meet a "Woman of Mystery"!

This month, we're proud to bring you another story in our ongoing WOMAN OF MYSTERY program, designed to bring you the debut books of writers new to Harlequin Intrigue.

Meet Laura Parker, author of *Indiscreet*.

Laura admits that she's a sucker for a good old-fashioned mystery. Says Laura, "I don't care that *The Maltese Falcon* has a plot so convoluted that by the end you don't know exactly who did what to whom or why. Give me atmosphere, clever dialogue and a strong, smart hero who against his better judgment just can't resist the mysterious woman 'with a past.' Oh, and please, a happy ending."

We're dedicated to bringing you the best new authors, the freshest new voices. Be on the lookout for more "Woman of Mystery" books!

Sincerely,

Debra Matteucci
Senior Editor and Editorial Coodinator
Harlequin Books
300 East 42nd Street
New York, New York 10017

Indiscreet
Laura Parker

Harlequin Books

TORONTO • NEW YORK • LONDON
AMSTERDAM • PARIS • SYDNEY • HAMBURG
STOCKHOLM • ATHENS • TOKYO • MILAN
MADRID • WARSAW • BUDAPEST • AUCKLAND

To Gary and Robin who were there when it really counted.

ISBN 0-373-22327-7

INDISCREET

Copyright © 1995 by Laura A. Castoro

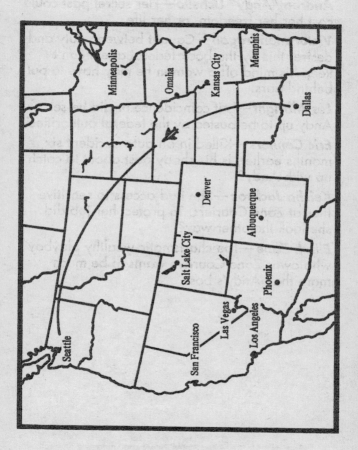

CAST OF CHARACTERS

Andrea "Andy" Uchello —Her secret past could cost her her freedom, or her life.

Victor Mondragon —Caught between duty and desire, this by-the-book federal agent can't keep his mind off a woman he may have to put behind bars.

Les Albright —Is it coincidence or did he set Andy up to be busted by the federal authorities?

Eric Conners —Killed in an auto accident six months earlier, is his shady past about to catch up with Andy?

Keisha Jackson —She had access to sensitive files at Zane Couriers. To protect her job did she look the other way?

Elijah Zane —The charismatic wealthy playboy who owns Zane Couriers wants to be much more than Andy's boss.

Prologue

An unfriendly smile hardened Victor Mondragon's features as he zeroed in on the man in aisle seat 13D. He was going to nail the bastard. He had gotten away twice before, and the last time he had made it personal. Victor didn't like it when business got personal.

For the moment, however, Victor blocked out the notion of settling old scores. Time for such things later, when his target was under arrest and cooling his heels in the tank.

As the jet taxied toward its takeoff position on the runway, the man in seat 13D opened his newspaper, unaware that this flight could be his last for a very long time. Victor told himself to relax. As long as they were aboard the plane his target was locked up as tightly as if he were already in custody. Yet tension was as much a part of his character as his drive to succeed on the job.

Victor glanced at the expensive watch strapped to his wrist, part of his disguise. He wore a hand-tailored Italian suit and shoes that fit his feet like gloves.

Not bad for a kid from the barrio, he thought. But the "look" of the barrio was one of the reasons he was given this assignment. At first glance he appeared to be a young tycoon, but further inspection yielded a different impression. His straight black hair was slicked back to a patent-leather gloss, he wore a heavy gold ID bracelet and too much cologne. These were grooming styles favored by Las Vegas bouncers, gigolos, underworld goons—hungry young men whose talents could be bought for the right money. His department had been trying for months to infiltrate an illegal courier ring. This time out, he was their point man.

Victor loved fieldwork. He didn't mind that it was often boring and repetitive, with success or failure hinging on the discovery or omission of a minute detail. He had patience to equal his drive. He didn't mind the long hours, the lack of sleep and praise, or the modest paycheck. It was old-fashioned pride in his work that motivated him. Twelve years ago he was headed toward a life in prison—or a quick, ugly death in the streets. Now he was a hunter, a protector, one of the good guys. It felt good. He felt good. He'd beaten the odds of his upbringing and escaped.

So, he had spent three lousy months trying to catch the scent of a cold trail while his colleagues had questioned the competence of his unit. Finally, his patience had paid off. The break had come in the form of a tip. The tip said Albright, who seldom did legwork, was "carrying" today. The informant was notorious for his unreliability but it had panned out.

Victor glanced out the window. So what if there'd been a last-minute seat assignment foul-up and he'd wound up in seat 14A instead of the still vacant 13F?

As soon as the pilot turned off the seat belt sign, he would exchange his seat for the open one next to his target, strike up a business acquaintance and then wait for the man to make a mistake. It was a done deal, a sure bet.

The engines roared and the plane shot off down the runway, the sudden acceleration pushing passengers back in their seats.

"Ooh!"

The sound was no more than an expulsion of breath but it distracted Victor. He turned and glanced down sharply. His seat companion, a four-year-old boy, was staring past him out the window as the world whizzed past in overdrive. The blood had deserted his face and his mouth hung ajar. Beneath a mop of blond curls his brown eyes were wide with fear. Victor recognized the signs of full-scale panic that was about to erupt into stereophonic sound.

To distract the boy, he stuck out a finger and waggled it under the huge stuffed purple dinosaur the boy had a stranglehold on. "That's a dangerous-looking creature you have there."

Victor smiled encouragingly at the boy who blinked and stared back at him in silence. Finally, the boy relaxed his death grip on the toy's neck and answered, "He's a dinosaur!"

Victor's brows rose in mock surprise and he snatched his hand back as the plane lifted off. "Does he bite?"

"Naw!" The boy's tone was full of grown-up contempt for such a foolish question but his grin said he was childishly delighted by the suggestion. "You want to hold him?"

Victor drew back in mock fear. "No, thanks." Another day he might have seen the humor in having a half-pint and his Paleolithic partner as seatmates. But the last thing he needed was a child between himself and his target.

Across the aisle the boy's mother offered him an apologetic smile. "I hope Lenny's not bothering you."

Victor shook his head and deliberately glanced back toward the window beyond which the ground was rapidly falling away. The woman had an infant in her arms who fretted as the plane banked in its steep climb. She looked as if she might need help—but he couldn't be it.

A moment later, a figure passed his row. Victor's attention shifted to her when she paused at row thirteen.

He noted first that her hands were empty and that there was no easy way for her to hide a weapon under that clingy dress. He also noted less important things like her youth, the generous curves of her slim body outlined by her sleeveless pale green knit dress, even the fine pair of legs revealed by her abbreviated hem. She seemed harmless enough, if a bit reckless, for they were still in a steep climb.

"You'd better sit down, Miss," an elderly man from the row directly ahead of Victor said as the young woman clung rather desperately to the back of the seat across the aisle.

She half turned toward the speaker and Victor saw the same panicky look of his young seatmate in her eyes. The alertness in him rekindled. Something was wrong.

Suddenly she spoke to the man in seat 13D. Victor couldn't hear her exact words, as the engines were still racing as the plane strained to gain altitude, but his target suddenly got up out of his seat.

Victor bit back a curse. What the hell was going on?

A flight attendant came charging up the aisle. Using an authoritarian tone, she launched into a well-rehearsed warning regarding passengers not moving about the cabin while the seat belt sign was still on.

Victor watched the woman passenger mouth what seemed to be an apology and smile nervously as the man stepped into the aisle to make way for her to enter his row. Then he spoke to the attendant. Victor caught only the tail end of his words, "...friends...sit together."

Friends? Victor's professional instincts went into overdrive. He knew his target's dossier by heart. The man usually worked alone. It was probably coincidence the woman had commandeered the seat he wanted. Yet, what if she was not merely a bit of bad timing but an accomplice? That might explain why she'd risked changing seats during takeoff. He needed to find out—before they landed—what was going on.

Victor reclined his seat, trying to get a better view of row thirteen. Aside from the man's profile, he couldn't see a thing. The woman had taken the seat by the window, which meant the middle seat was still vacant. Yet, he couldn't think of a single reasonable excuse to use to explain why he might want to wedge himself into that seat between them. A desperate or obviously stupid move would cost him his credibility. He had to face the truth. His chance had been blown, for now.

He glared up at the still illuminated seat belt sign. He should have ignored it just as the woman had. But he was a by-the-book kind of guy.

When the chime sounded and the seat belt light was finally turned off, Victor looked down at the boy beside him. "How'd you like to look out the window, Lenny?" His gaze flicked upward toward the boy's mother, who was glancing anxiously his way. She had been in the midst of changing a diaper. Victor gave her his Sunday-best smile. "Would you mind if Lenny and I changed seats?"

"I suppose not...not if he really wants to," she answered hesitantly, searching Victor's expression. He supposed she was trying to decide if he was as kind as he seemed or a rather personable child molester. He didn't blame her. He knew firsthand that dangerous people came in all colors, shapes and guises. "Sure, why not," she finished with a shrug.

Victor raised the armrests between them and then hoisted Lenny over his lap as he slid into the aisle seat. Once he had belted the boy in and made a few soothing comments, he sat back, closed his eyes and began to listen.

His fellow officers attributed his keen hearing to the "Cherokee" blood flowing in his veins. They ignored the fact that his features and coloring were a product of his Salvadoran mother and Spanish father. As for his listening skills, they came from practice. He trained that concentration now on the two voices across the aisle and one row up.

Three and a half long weary hours later, Victor was no more certain than before about the nature of the relationship between the couple in row thirteen. They certainly were chummy. They had talked nearly nonstop, often with their heads bent toward each other, about the weather in the Caribbean this time of year, current foreign films, sushi and chic nightspots in Dallas. It seemed they shared expensive tastes. Or, maybe they were just flirting. At the very least the young woman was doing her best to keep his target's interest. Some men had all the luck with pretty women.

He heard her laughter again rise gently above the cabin noise. The pleasant sound had a smoky quality to it, and he felt it curl playfully along his spine, unforgettable and instantly recognizable. Not a good trait for a person in the same line of work as her seatmate. More than likely it was mere coincidence that she had chosen to sit next to him. But he didn't operate on probabilities. He'd have to take precautions.

Fifteen minutes out from Dallas/Fort Worth International Airport, Victor made his move. He went forward to use the lavatory, ignoring the scowl of the flight attendant who disapproved of him using the first-class facilities. As he came back down the aisle a few minutes later, he met the inquiring glance of his partner, Phil, who sat in first class. As their gazes met, he made a V with his fingers. It was their code for the number two. Before lowering his hand, he added a third finger, all pointing upward. III was code for "W": woman. Phil frowned but nodded once and then reached for the phone on the seat back ahead of him. Phil would see to it the guys on the ground in Dallas were prepared.

It seemed an eternity before the plane came to a stop at the gate. Victor shot to his feet, ready to move quickly. A moment later, his target's companion came to her feet and turned to look straight toward him.

Victor looked away, not wanting to make eye contact. Still, he had seen enough to confirm that she was as attractive as her voice. Nor did he miss seeing his target place a familiar hand at the small of her back as she brushed past him into the aisle. He ignored the

urge to help her as she stretched up on tiptoe to retrieve her bag from the overhead compartment.
Ahead, he saw his partner step into the aisle as passengers began shuffling toward the exit. He cut his
eyes deliberately toward the suspect as Phil glanced
back.

"Excuse me. Would you mind?"

Victor turned and looked into the face of the young
mother, who was struggling to extract a folded stroller
from the overhead. For a fraction of a second annoyance warred with civility. He didn't want to lose his
target and the couple was moving away.

"Sure." He took down the stroller and opened it,
leaving it blocking the aisle as he hurried away.

As Victor exited the gate he saw that his targets had
paused a few yards away and were in earnest conversation. For reasons he couldn't explain he hoped she'd
just walk away from the man, and trouble. Instead, he
saw the man tear a ribbon of paper off his ticket and
hand it to her. He bit back an expletive. It was a luggage claim. Albright was passing on his illegal merchandise to her. Was she his contact after all? For an
instant longer the pair exchanged warm intimate
smiles as other passengers surged past them. Then they
parted, the man moving in one direction while the
woman headed in the opposite, toward baggage claim.

Phil stood on the far side of the walkway by the
men's room, his arms folded casually. Victor jerked a
thumb in the woman's direction and mouthed, "Pick
her up," then turned to follow the man. The guy was
making a beeline for a bank of telephones. Something was definitely up. And he'd bet his badge the
woman was in it up to her pretty little neck.

Chapter One

"Please start again at the beginning, Ms. Uchello."

Andrea Uchello gripped her foam cup tighter, making it squeak as the muted sound of jet engines swelled momentarily overhead. The man seated across from her wore a uniform. She focused on his badge: Airport Security: Adam Lowell. For the past hour she had been sitting in this stark, windowless room trying to explain to him and the uniformed female officer by the door, why she had picked up another person's briefcase at baggage claim. Her palms were sweating, her brow was damp, and beneath her pale green bouclé knit dress her body was slick with perspiration. She had run the emotional gamut from shock and embarrassment at being detained straight through to fear and intimidation during this questioning. Now Andy was rapidly regaining her natural confidence, and with it her temper.

"We've been over and over this," she said in the clipped tone she often used to cover her more volatile feelings. "I don't know what else I can say."

"The way to help yourself, Ms. Uchello, is to cooperate with us," Adam Lowell replied in a calm but insistent tone.

Andy's outrage at the injustice of her situation flared. "I am cooperating. If you don't believe my version of what happened then ask the owner of the bag."

"We are asking *you*," replied a male voice from somewhere behind her right shoulder.

Andy sucked in a breath of surprise. She had forgotten there was another person present. A man had slipped into the room behind her half an hour ago and had been standing silently just out of her range of vision ever since. As she turned her head to look at him, Officer Lowell said curtly, "Please remain facing forward, Ms. Uchello."

Andy obeyed, but she did not appreciate anyone giving her orders. She had never responded well to authority. More than once her rebellious nature had gotten her into trouble. But this time she was innocent. They were the ones who should be doing the explaining.

The man behind her spoke again. "We don't have all day, Ms. Uchello. If you'd rather the matter was turned over to the police, we can see that you're escorted downtown."

The police! Every hair on her nape bristled and Andy automatically lifted a hand to brush away the annoying sensation. She most definitely didn't want to deal with the police. Yet, from somewhere deep inside, remnants of the cocky rebellious teenager she had once been surfaced. That bullying tone wasn't going to intimidate her. Besides, she was innocent of...why they hadn't even told her why she was being questioned!

She tamped down her temper. She was no longer a hotheaded teen who couldn't judge when she was making a bad situation worse. Stories of people being arrested for merely joking about bombs or guns within the hearing of airport security officials made her reconsider being uncooperative. These people were serious. And she had a lot—maybe everything—to lose.

She recrossed her legs and sat back in an attempt to make herself relax. "All right. Once more for the record. I met a man on the plane. He seemed nice enough. Said he was from Chicago, a businessman. We chatted during the flight. When we landed he said he needed to make a phone call. He gave me his luggage stub and asked if I would mind picking up his case if it came up on the carousel before he arrived. We had already agreed to split the cost of a cab because we're both staying downtown."

"Do you often pick up strange men?" inquired The Voice.

"I did not pick him up," Andy said curtly. "We happened to be seated next to each other on the flight."

"The seating plan says otherwise." Lowell reached for his clipboard and looked at it. "You were given seat 21B. The gentleman you described was assigned a seat in row thirteen. You changed seats."

"Right." Andy doggedly held on to her temper. If she started making even innocent mistakes about the details of her story, she would never get out of here. "As I explained earlier, I wanted a window and I'd been stuck in a middle seat." She offered him the first smile of the interview. Men usually found her smiles charming. "I have this irrational belief that the earth will disappear if I can't keep an eye on it. You know. Fear of flying."

"So you *chose* to sit next to him." The Voice crackled with sarcasm. "Was it because he was attractive?"

If anyone else asked her that question—a colleague or a girlfriend—she would have told the truth. But she wasn't going to admit that the man's looks played any part in her choice of seats. "He didn't look like an ax murderer, if that's what you mean," she said in a hostile tone.

"What about a smuggler?"

Andy felt her stomach spasm. "A drug dealer?" How was she to have guessed that the Louis Vuitton briefcase she had hoisted off the luggage carousel in the spirit of friendliness contained contraband? After all, it was a domestic flight. Weren't drugs only smuggled into or out of a country?

"What makes you think we found drugs, Ms. Uchello?"

Officer Lowell's question startled Andy, who'd been unaware that she had spoken her thoughts aloud. "Well, wasn't it drugs?" she asked.

"Is that what he told you?" asked The Voice.

By an act of great will she kept from turning her head toward her accuser. "Oh, right! A stranger on a plane tells me he's a criminal and I say, 'Oh, please, please, let me be involved.'"

"Bravado won't help you," The Voice replied. "What did you say his name was?"

"Les."

"Les what?"

Andy inhaled sharply. "Just Les. We didn't exchange business cards or phone numbers. It's three and a half hours from New York to Dallas. Sometimes you talk to the person next to you. If he'd done or said anything the least bit suspicious, you'd be talking to someone else. Damn it! I'm sorry I ever touched the bag!"

"There's no need to shout, Miss," Officer Lowell said calmly.

But Andy was past being calm. There was just so much she could take. "Oh, isn't there? I made a mistake. People make mistakes."

"Some mistakes can be costly," came the laconic reply from the rear of the room. "Jail is a high price to pay for stupidity."

"That's it!" Andy jumped up from her seat and turned on her tormentor. Through the lens of her anger-distorted gaze, he was merely a tall, square-shouldered blur. "Since when is it against the law to be stupid? I've been detained, embarrassed—no, publicly humiliated—and accused of some unspecified crime I didn't even know was being committed. I think that's about the limit of what the law allows authorities to do to the stupid."

"Sit down."

The moment he spoke her vision cleared in a blink of surprise. He was tall with black mink hair combed straight back to hug his head like a pelt. Long black lashes provided a veranda for eyes so gold they seemed catlike. Deep bronze skin stretched over the architecture of a face that made words like attractive or handsome seem inadequate. What might be a fine masculine mouth was tight with emotions she did not have to guess at. He was as angry as she was. But who was he?

Her eyes strayed from his face. He didn't wear a uniform or a badge. He was smartly dressed in what she recognized as an Italian designer suit. She doubted a plainclothes policeman would have so extravagant a budget. Maybe she had picked up the wrong piece of luggage—his luggage. Was that it?

"Sit down, Ms. Uchello." His tone implied insubordination in the ranks.

She looked up and met his gaze. This was not a man accustomed to repeating himself. But she was not the sort of woman who reacted well to orders. The rebel in her needed venting. She suspected the next words were going to cost her but, whatever else he might be, he was rude and she didn't like rude people. She summoned what was left of her dignity and said, "I'm sorry, but you haven't yet identified yourself."

For one incredible second Andy thought he might use physical coercion to make her sit, so volatile did he seem. And yet, as she forced herself to hold the stare in those unfriendly eyes, she sensed that he was calculating his effect on her in the full confidence that the mere threat of his anger would be sufficient intimidation. It was a raw moment: her female audacity pitched against his implacable male authority.

The tingle of a blush began behind her ears and then quickly mantled her cheeks. The quickening excitement inside her had nothing to do with embarrassment or fear. The thrill of her defiance came from another, totally different source—it was purely sexual. He was gorgeous, dark, sensuous and glowing with the kind of charged sensuality you could see rolling down the road even on a dark night. He reminded her of a very expensive sports car—sleek, powerful and potentially dangerous in the hands of the inexperienced.

She saw his eyes widen slightly in mutual awareness, the pithy pupils engulfing his liquid gold irises. That tiny triumph made her want to smile. She liked danger, always had. But this time she couldn't afford the price of admission.

She turned toward Officer Lowell. "Look. You can't hold me without any charges. If nothing else, I'm entitled to an attorney's presence."

"You'll need a damned good one if you aren't telling the truth," the man behind her said in a tone made all the more disturbing by the fact that it was delivered as a whisper deposited into her right ear.

Andy braced herself with both hands on the tabletop, refusing to acknowledge his presence so close to her. She addressed Lowell. "I demand to know what I'm being accused of. And I demand to use the phone."

She saw Lowell exchange glances with the man behind her, whose presence registered like radiant heat along every inch of her back.

"Very well, Ms. Uchello. Make your call. There's a phone in the next room. Be certain it's local."

Andy straightened. "Thank you."

But before she could move toward the door the man behind her said, "I have one more question."

Andy turned to face him but focused on the wall just above his left shoulder. "You've chosen a strange profession for a woman who has a phobia about flying."

Andy adjusted her line of vision to square with the middle of his chest. He held an eel-skin pad in one hand. He read from it, "Bonded courier. Flies twice a week on the average." He looked up at her, his gaze two glints of gold between twin thickets of sable. "It must pay awfully well."

Though she doubted she would ever see him again, she knew the look in those gold eyes would remain imprinted on her mind for some time to come. For that reason alone, she refused to be civil. "I have nothing else to say."

He flipped his pad closed. "Make your call, Ms. Uchello." As if he had dismissed her, he turned away. It was then she noticed yet another unexpected detail—his thick hair ended in a short neat ponytail.

When she had left the room, followed by the female officer, Officer Lowell turned to the other man in the room. "Pretty gal."

"Pretty but foolish."

"Is that your professional opinion, Mister Mondragon?"

Victor merely smiled and reached for the pad of notes Lowell had taken while Ms. Uchello spoke. But he did not immediately begin to read.

He liked women, liked them all: short and bouncy, tall and willowy, curvacious or athletic; blond, brunette, or redhead. His male friends, who all had definite shopping lists of female attributes, liked to joke that he had no taste. What he had was a generous, broad-minded appreciation of the profundity of womanhood. Yet, early in his career, a pretty felon had made a fool of him by sweet-talking him into allowing her to use a public rest room. She'd escaped, leaving him to explain to his superiors how he'd lost her. He'd never made that mistake again and had quickly gained a reputation for being tough, thorough, and nearly impossible to deceive.

He took nothing at face value. He let others do the talking when a suspect was brought in for questioning. He had learned that he could often judge more from body language than from facial expressions. A professional criminal knew how to lie, and lie well. The telltale swinging leg, tapping foot or involuntary muscle twitch that might go unnoticed when standing face-to-face frequently became a revealing character trait if viewed impartially. Usually he came away with a dispassionate judgment, but not a lingering impression of the person.

It had almost worked with Andrea Uchello. If she had not turned on him in anger, he might not have carried away any other impression of her beyond the fact that she was quite a looker. And that her laughter blew smoke rings through his thoughts.

Oh, he'd been aware of her as a woman, with her expensive, subtly suggestive perfume. He'd also noticed that her short dark hair lay in feathery curls along her cheeks just like Audrey Hepburn's in *Sabrina,* which he'd been watching between 2:00 and 4:00 a.m. the night before because he couldn't sleep— again. If that were not enough, her one unconscious betrayal of nervousness had been to keep crossing and recrossing her legs, until just the whisper of her stockings fascinated him.

But then she'd stood up and faced him, and the unexpected intelligence and fury in her dark eyes had radically altered his perception of her. He suspected righteous indignation had never come in a prettier or sexier package. She was no longer just another attractive woman. Suddenly, she was registering directly on all his senses. Her small, firm breasts had thrust gently toward him as though they were just what he had ordered. Her voice, which he had listened to here and on the plane as only the conveyor of information, pleasantly stirred something deep within him when she spoke directly to him. Even the scent of her perfume seemed to alter. Charged with the extra frisson of her own body's unique chemistry, it rose from the heated surface of her skin and wafted in behind his breath, smoking his mind with purely sexual imaginings. It had made him want to touch her....

For about the dozenth time this week he was sorry he'd given up smoking, which he'd done just after he broke up with Catherine. Seven months of no sex and no cigarettes.

Get a grip! Victor sucked in a hard, sobering breath. So what if he was feeling amorous? So what if the realities of modern life couldn't keep him from being unhappy about his self-inflicted deprivation? Perhaps, that was why he was fantasizing about possibilities—like Andrea Uchello. In any case, he had a job to do.

"Well, what do you think?"

Victor looked up from the unread pad to greet his partner, Phil, who had entered the room. "I think it's possible she's a dupe. It's not uncommon for people carrying contraband to enlist the help of unsuspecting parties. Albright never intended to meet her at the cabstand. He took the airport shuttle into town without even looking for her. Damn! How much luck can one man have? You think Albright smelled us closing in on him?"

"He does seem to have a sixth sense," Phil Symes agreed and nodded in acknowledgment of Officer Lowell.

"You Feds been trailing this guy long?" Lowell inquired, hoping for more details.

"Seven months," Victor replied, his tone sour.

Lowell wagged his head in sympathy. "Losing your chance to nail him has got to smart."

"Not as much as losing an agent," Phil replied.

"What happened?"

Phil glanced at Victor who nodded his approval. "Three months ago, one of our men was following Albright, whom we suspect was ferrying drug money down to the Cayman Islands for laundering." Phil shrugged. "Guess he got careless."

"That won't happen again." Victor glanced over at Phil. "I think I've figured out how to correct our mistake."

"Why is it I have the feeling your method's going to cause a ripple in the ranks?" Phil answered with a frank grin.

Victor didn't answer. He would rather cause a few ripples than make excuses. He didn't like excuses. He took full responsibility for the botched mission. The department had waited a long time for the opportunity to bust the most successful operation of illegal couriers in the country. He had been aboard the flight to shadow Albright, to pose as a courier himself and perhaps even lure Albright into trying to recruit him. That was why he was wearing a suit worth the entire contents of his own personal wardrobe. The expensive Italian shoes, extravagant gold watch and the wad of hundred dollar bills in his wallet were all part of his cover. But he hadn't planned on the brunette in a pixie haircut eliminating his options.

While he had followed Albright, who had first made a phone call and then left the airport on the shuttle bus, Phil had nabbed Ms. Uchello picking up a case containing stolen securities. He'd let Albright go because he had no reason to stop him. Ms. Uchello was another matter. He had yet to decide officially whether she was Albright's associate or merely an innocent bystander. He rather hoped she was the latter, even though she fit the profile of the former.

He glanced again at Lowell's notes. She had expensive tastes, wore expensive clothes, and her job status belied the fact that she could easily afford such luxuries. She was young, pretty and not easily rattled. Her security clearance as a bonded courier would be a valuable asset to a man in Albright's trade. Experience had proved to him that many a foolish young woman had gotten roped into criminal activity by the desire for the better things in life. He hoped Andrea Uchello was stronger than that.

Not that it should matter to him what her history was. She was not his first concern. If Albright suspected they were on to him, he would go underground and the Treasury Department would have to start all over again, looking for another illegal courier to track. His department had already lost one man in pursuit. He had to salvage his assignment. So he would do what any man would when backed to the wall—he would work with what had come to hand.

Victor looked up at Officer Lowell. "Would you mind keeping Ms. Uchello occupied outside a moment longer? Get her coffee or a soda, whatever she'd like."

Lowell came reluctantly to his feet for he knew he was being dismissed. "Sure thing."

When he left, Victor turned to Phil. "Now, here's what we're going to do."

Chapter Two

Andy hugged her arms to her chest as she leaned intently toward Jim Lawson, a Dallas-based attorney who was also a business client of her courier firm. "They can't charge me, can they?"

"They can try." Jim's usually genial expression was blank, professional. He had just been briefed by airport security and from the look on his face, what he had been told wasn't good news. "In any event, they can make your life miserable for the next few days."

Andy bit her lip. She had demanded to know what crime she was being accused of committing. Now that she knew, she wished she was still in ignorance. "Possession of stolen bank securities. I can't believe it."

"Believe it." Jim nodded when she glanced in annoyance at him. "I saw the report. It's no joke, Andy. The briefcase you picked up contained stolen goods. That makes you an accessory after the fact—a part of the theft."

"I know what it means!" Andy heard the edge in her voice and stood up to pace, giving physical expression to her anxiety. She knew better than most the penalty for being named an accessory to a crime, and that was the trouble. She couldn't stand the thought of being arrested, arraigned, held without bond. No, that mustn't happen. Her life would shatter like dropped crystal.

"Andy, is there something you're not telling me?"

She turned abruptly and gave Jim a not-quite-convincing smile. "You've known me for two years, Jim. If you thought I was capable of criminal activity, would you have asked that I be assigned as the regular courier for your law office?"

She saw sympathy enter his expression, and just a smidgen of doubt. "The attorney-client privilege is confidential, Andy."

She gave him an injured, incredulous look. He did doubt her! She shrugged and cast a pleading look in his direction. "You know what a perfectionist I am. An overdraft on my bank account makes me break out in hives. The very idea of scandal, it's unthinkable!" She approached him, offering a scant smile. "There's got to be something you can do to get me out of this mess."

He glanced at the door where, beyond the narrow off-center rectangle of glass, a Dallas policeman's khaki sleeve was visible. "I can advise you not to consider any offer they've made thus far."

"Offer?" Relief made her shoulders relax. "What do they want me to do, identify the man from mug shots?" Her smile widened. "Let me at them. I need to get out of here. I'm booked for another out-of-town assignment this week."

Jim looked pained. "I wouldn't count on doing much work until this is settled. Being held on suspicion of a crime could cancel your bonded credentials."

Andy stiffened again. "Who's going to tell my employers?"

Jim merely nodded at the door.

"They said that? They threatened my job?" All the hot emotion ebbed out of her, leaving her chilled and feeling exposed. She turned to stare at the closed door as if she could see right through it to the men who had been interrogating her. When she turned back to Jim all the frustration and uncertainty she had been hiding were on plain view in her expression. "Why? What, exactly, do they want me to do?"

Jim came to his feet. "There's no point in discussing it. It's not an offer I'd even let you consider."

"Why not?"

Both of them jumped at the sound of Victor Mondragon's voice. He had opened the door without making a sound and was leaning through the breach. "We're short on time, Mr. Lawson. Why don't you let Ms. Uchello decide for herself?"

Andy crossed her arms below her bosom, welcoming the return of her anger. "Since I don't know what I'm being asked to do, I can't decide anything."

Victor's black brows drew together as he stepped inside and shut the door. "Didn't your lawyer tell you the deal?"

"I did not."

Victor watched in amusement as the attorney moved forward, as if in standing beside his client he was somehow protecting her. "What you're asking my client to do is risky. It could even be dangerous. She's a victim, not a criminal. You can't expect her to involve herself any further."

Victor's golden gaze drifted from the lawyer to Andy and remained. "Don't you even want to hear the offer?"

"Why don't *you* tell me?" Andy demanded.

Victor reached back and reopened the door. "If your attorney will step outside a moment, I'll be glad to."

"I must protest—" Jim began but Andy lay a hand on his arm.

"It's okay, Jim. The offer can't hurt me."

"I should remain, for your sake," Jim maintained.

"You can remain by the door, if you'd like, so you won't miss Ms. Uchello's cry for help," Victor offered dryly.

Andy sent Jim a reassuring smile. "I'll be okay."

When he had shut the door on the lawyer, Victor turned and leaned back against it, slipping both hands into his pockets. For a moment he sized up Andrea Uchello.

While she had waited for her attorney he had read the results of a routine check on her, which revealed among other things that she was twenty-five, single, and was born in a town called Yard, Texas, population 361. He was intrigued. The world didn't get much smaller than Yard, Texas. Yet, there was nothing homespun about her. From the top of her chic haircut to the toes of her elegant shoes, she was one class act. Whatever Texas accent she might've had was long since replaced by a refined and deliberate manner of speech—all-American and non-regional. The question was, had the same drive that turned a small-town girl into a world-class woman led her into a life of crime?

He didn't like what he was about to do. He was good at his job. Breaking down defenses was his specialty, but he didn't find it pleasant work. Still, she had involved herself in federal matters, and he couldn't afford to be wrong about her. "I want you to find your friend Les and hand over the case."

"Just like that?" She seemed stunned.

Victor nodded once. "Just like that."

Annoyance flicked through her reply. "I don't know where to find him."

"Did you give him your address?"

"No. I planned to spend a night at the Adolphus."

Victor's gaze narrowed. "You gave as your residence a Dallas address. Why stay at a hotel?"

"Sometimes I like to treat myself to a night of luxury," she said defensively. "Some people buy season tickets to the Cowboys' games. I prefer the occasional breakfast in bed."

He whistled softly. "Expensive tastes." He emphasized the word *expensive* to goad her. His gaze slipped pointedly over her designer knit dress to her lizard shoes. *Go after her,* he told himself. *She thinks she's tough. Scratch the surface and see what comes out.* "Is Les staying at the Adolphus, too? Adjoining rooms, maybe?"

"You're rude. I don't like rude men," she said flatly. "The gentleman said he was staying at the Sheraton."

Victor smiled at her description of his target as a gentleman—as opposed to his own conduct, he supposed. She had no idea just how ungentlemanly he could be but she would soon find out if she didn't cooperate. "You see? You do know where to find him."

She seemed taken aback by his answer. Had she really forgotten that bit of information, or was she that good of an actress?

Andy felt the dread of being slowly bound in an invisible silken web. "Look. I didn't ask to be part of this mess. Why should I help you?"

"Because you blew my investigation sky-high this afternoon. You owe me."

"I owe you?" One of her perfectly arched mahogany brows cocked upwards. "Isn't theft of securities a federal offense?"

"I'm a Fed."

She gave his Italian designer suit the once-over. "In Ferragamo? So, that's where my tax dollars go." She paused a beat. "I'm not impressed."

Tough and funny. His admiration for her self-possession was growing with each moment. He pulled his right hand out of his pocket and rotated his wrist to glance at the twenty-four-karat gold timepiece spanning his wrist. He saw her eyes widen as she spied it. Was it disapproval or covetousness? "I'll level with you because in an hour your yes or no won't matter." He straightened away from the wall and came toward her.

He didn't pause as he reached her but took her by the arm and propelled her along with him toward the sofa at the end of the room. "Sit down," he said and, without waiting for her to comply, pulled her down close beside him.

He leaned forward until he was inhaling the seductive fragrance rising from her satin-smooth skin. When she looked at him, he saw the twin images of himself reflected in her dark eyes. "Here's the deal. I was on that flight with you this afternoon. Yeah, I know," he continued at her look of surprise, "you only had eyes for Albright. Well, your friend is a courier, too. Only he delivers and picks up illegal goods. We learned that old Les was carrying today. It was my job to strike up an acquaintance in the hope of infiltrating his ring." His expression sobered. "Then you showed up and derailed my plans."

"You're an undercover man?" she asked.

"Something like that." She was so close he could see the pulse fluttering in the shallow between her collar bones. *Stay focused, Victor!* We've arrested a few couriers, but it turned out they were hired freelance and couldn't tell us anything about their employer. We think Albright may be the brains behind the ring."

"Why not arrest him?"

"We're going to do that but we hoped he'd lead us through the inner workings of the operation first."

She frowned and he wondered if she was aware of the tantalizing brush of her shoulder against his arm as he rested a hand on the sofa back. "So, you're FBI?" she asked at last.

He smiled and it drew her eyes to his mouth. Hers, he noted, was quite full when not tensed by anger. "Securities thefts are the Treasury Department's bailiwick."

She leaned back against the Naugahyde upholstery, putting a little breathing distance between them. Her gaze was mocking but still wary. "Are you serious?"

"Treasury agent, Victor Mondragon. I specialize in tracking stolen bonds and securities." He had to resist the urge to touch the thin gold necklace encircling her throat. She looked so inviting, soft and delicate. He shifted uncomfortably. This cozy chat was affecting him more strongly than he realized.

He watched her edge back a fraction more as she turned her head to glance at the door. He knew what she was thinking, that maybe she should have had an attorney present.

Before he could stop himself, he moved the hand he had braced on the sofa behind her head to brush the scattering of S-hook curls that lay against her neck below her left ear. As her head whipped back toward him, he saw that her eyes were narrowed by suspicion and then he spied the blossoming of color where his fingers had grazed her skin. The blush didn't please him. Never mind that his ego was flattered by her reaction and that his anatomy was responding to expectations that could not be met. She was a suspect and regulations didn't allow fraternizing with suspects under interrogation.

He moved away from her, certain he had crossed the invisible barrier of professional conduct. Oh, but she was soft, with hair like silk and skin soft as a child's.

Andy turned her head away to better regroup her scattered thoughts. He was playing some sort of flirtatious game with her but she didn't understand its purpose. "I don't see what any of this has to do with me. If you know all about Les Albright, then you know I have no connection to him."

"Can you prove it?"

Andy's head swiveled toward him. "I beg your pardon?"

"I said, can you prove it?"

"But you just said—"

His tone was calm, direct, impersonal. "What I said was that I was prepared to offer my services to a known black-market courier. What I don't know is whether or not you've made the same deal."

Andy shot to her feet. "This is ridiculous! I never saw that man before in my life."

He stood up as well. "Can you prove that?" He leaned closer, his superior height adding weight to his words. "Can you prove that you don't know Les Albright? Can you prove that you didn't know you were retrieving stolen merchandise with his luggage? Can you prove that you aren't already in Albright's pocket?"

Andy stared in amazement at him. "You can't *prove* otherwise."

His voice remained low and unemotional but his handsome face suddenly looked quite brutal. "I can make your life hell while I try."

"That's blackmail," she whispered, almost afraid to acknowledge what she was hearing. She held his gaze but her chin betrayed with a tremor her first real moment of fear. While he did not yet know it, *she* knew she couldn't afford to have him dig into her background. She had plenty of reasons to dislike lawmen, federal agents in particular. Men with badges didn't care whom they hurt, or how they hurt people, if it meant they got what they were after. Years ago a federal agent's callous tactics had ruined her life. Now this fed wanted her to stick her neck out again. No way. Not ever!

The old hatred blazed up, burning in her eyes. And yet a hard fist of fear deeper down made her whisper, "Why are you doing this to me?"

The sudden note of fear in her voice surprised Victor. He shook his head slightly to dispel the sense that he had gone too far and was needlessly bullying her. Her vulnerability could not stop him, even if it pained him. "The fact is you were arrested in possession of stolen merchandise. If I was innocent, and some stranger had gotten me mixed up in his mess, I'd want to see him caught. You can cooperate with us or you can refuse. It's up to you."

He wasn't bluffing, she saw that clearly. "And if I refuse? You'd wreck my life, knowing I'm innocent?"

"I don't know for a fact that you're innocent. You can show good faith by cooperating, or you can go downtown and be booked." He glanced at his watch and then shrugged. "It's only 5:30. I'm certain your lawyer can have you out on bail by midnight."

"Dear God!" she said softly. She had been detained for three hours. Now she was just minutes from being under arrest. She must not, could not, allow that to happen. Yet cooperating meant helping a federal agent, something she'd vowed never to do again. The impotence of her position made her tremble.

Victor watched her impassively. She looked thoroughly shaken by the prospect of being jailed, even for a few hours. He'd known hardened criminals to react the same way. Being locked up terrorized otherwise heartless souls. Yet, her reaction made him feel like a bully all the same. What he had told her was true. He had begun to believe that she was innocent but her fate wasn't up to him. So there it was. He had to press her, however distasteful the idea was to him personally.

Andy found her voice. "Why don't you just simply turn the case into the airport's Lost and Found?" A hopeful smile hovered around her mouth. "People do it all the time, leave bags unclaimed. Albright would assume I never picked it up."

"Sorry, no." Victor admired her effort. But life was never as simple as it seemed. What he was reluctant to

tell her, or her lawyer, was that if Albright learned or
even suspected she had been detained by the authorities, her life could be in danger. If Albright had deliberately left a fortune in stolen securities in the hands
of an unsuspecting woman, he would expect her to
have them—untouched—when he turned up. Anything else would signal Albright that his operation had
been compromised. Personally, he dreaded the idea of
putting a civilian at risk. But circumstances had left
him with no alternative. He had to make certain that
Albright felt safe. Sometimes, he hated this job.

"I need your answer, Ms. Uchello."

Fear tightened the icy knot inside Andy, freezing out
her confusion and resentment. If she didn't cooperate, he would have her arrested. The life she had spent
years very carefully reconstructing from the ashes of
a harrowing adolescence would be ruined. What else
could she expect from a man who made his living ha-
rassing criminals?

She stared at him, her hatred taking on a personal
edge. Behind the sexy physique and killer smile of
Victor Mondragon lay the ruthless nature of a federal
agent. She was going to cooperate because she had no
choice.

Yet fear of retribution wasn't the only reason she
was going to cooperate. Les Albright had traded on
her gullibility and she was in deep trouble because of
it. When was she going to learn that all men were rats?

"I'll cooperate," she said, her voice full of ani-
mosity. "But not because you threatened me. I don't
happen to like being taken for a fool."

No other answer could have pleased Victor more. In
spite of the pressure he had exerted on her emotions,
she had zeroed in on the real culprit. The only re-

maining question was, could she competently handle
Albright? He hoped she held on to her anger. It might
help get her through the next few hours.

"Think of this as your patriotic duty, Ms. Uchello.
Kind of like serving jury duty."

He smiled, but nothing Andy saw in his expression
was the least bit reassuring. In fact, her resentment
grew in exact proportion to his attractiveness.

She smoothed a hand over her cheek then tucked a
feathering of curls behind her ear. "If this is your idea
of patriotism, I won't be buying any more Treasury
bills."

FIFTEEN MINUTES LATER Andy sat in a cab heading
downtown, the dreaded Louis Vuitton attaché case
leaning against her calf. After a halfhearted attempt
to refresh her makeup, she snapped her compact shut
with a sigh.

"You look great."

Andy ignored her companion's comment. Agent
Mondragon had sent a watchdog along. To keep her
company, he had said. More likely to spy on her.

"I know you've had a hard day. You can relax
now."

Andy finally turned her head toward the pleasant-
faced young man with sandy hair and a neat mus-
tache. "What did you say your name was again?"

"Phil Symes."

"And you're—"

"An associate of Victor's," he cut in, and looked
meaningfully from her toward the cabdriver.

"How long have you known Mister Mondragon?"
Andy asked, curious to know something about the
man who held her future in his hands.

"Victor and I have worked together since we joined the department six years ago," Phil said proudly. "You can count on our professionalism, Ms. Uchello. We'll take care of everything. Victor sweats the details so others don't have to. It will all be over before you know it."

Andy didn't answer. The very last thing she wanted was Victor Mondragon expending his considerable talents scrutinizing her life. A moment later the cab pulled up to their destination.

The Adolphus Hotel was one of Dallas's oldest and grandest. Andy had been looking forward to staying here since the moment she'd been given the go-ahead by her client to make the reservation. From the liveried doorman to the completely refurbished lobby, every detail was meant to conjure up original turn-of-the-century splendor. Within minutes of arriving she knew her expectations of impeccable service and true luxury were justified. The carpets were plush underfoot, her check-in accomplished with amazing ease.

As they rode the elevator, the bellboy chatted amiably about the sights a visitor should see while in Dallas, pointing out the delights of the newest exhibition at the Dallas Museum of Art, the evening programs at the world-class Meyerson Symphony Hall, and then listing a few of the dining possibilities in the West End or in more trendy Deep Ellum, depending on one's taste. Andy fed him questions to keep from having to answer any of his.

When he opened the door to her room, she stood a moment in amazement. This was no ordinary room, this was a suite, complete with sitting room.

"I think there's been a mistake," Andy began as the bellboy wheeled in her baggage.

He paused and looked at his key. "It's no mistake, ma'am," he said with a grin.

"But I didn't ask for a suite, I asked for a single room."

"Compliments of Mister Mondragon," Phil Symes offered from the doorway.

Andy frowned at him. "I don't want any favors."

Phil shrugged. "Boss's orders. Enjoy." He waited until the bellboy had carried in her bags and then tipped him before Andy could protest. "You know where to reach us," Phil reminded her. "Have a pleasant evening."

Chapter Three

Andy slipped off her heels and padded across the sitting room to the huge arrangement of fruit and cheese on the dining table. The note said "Compliments of the Adolphus."

Smiling for the first time in hours, she plucked a grape and stuck it in her mouth. The skin popped easily, flooding her palate with sweet juice. "Delish!" she exclaimed and reached for another.

"We aim to please."

She turned toward the entrance, a look of surprise dawning on her face when she did not see anyone standing there.

"Over here, Ms. Uchello."

Ninety degrees left of the main door, Victor Mondragon, minus his jacket and tie, stood in another open doorway.

"Who let you in?" she asked and popped another grape in her mouth to cover a sudden onset of nerves.

He held up a hotel key. "We're roommates."

Andy nearly choked on her grape.

He grinned. "You can close me out by locking your side of the double doors, but I wouldn't advise it."

"Who cares?" she answered and came directly toward him. "My life's my own, once I've delivered the goods. Isn't that what you G-men would say?"

"T-men. I'm a T-man."

"How clever. Do you all have alphabet names?"

He propped a forearm high on the door frame and the action stretched his long torso, drawing his dress shirt taut across his abdomen and chest. Silk, Andy thought as she neared him. That would explain why the fabric clung like cellophane to every swell and ripple of muscle beneath it. Even the smoky shadow of dark male nipples could be glimpsed through the translucent silk. He had crossed his legs at the ankles, and where his trousers creased at the crotch, it was hard to miss the fact that Victor Mondragon was an impressively built man.

She stopped just far enough away not to seem intimidated but not so close as to seem drawn in by his blatant sexuality. She reached for her door intending to close it, in his face if necessary. "Get out."

He looked past her. "Don't you like your accommodations? You said you had a weakness for luxury."

Her eyes narrowed as she held the door. "I always pay the tab when I indulge my weaknesses. I don't think I can afford your kind of generosity."

He nodded his head and moved away from the door into her room. "Okay, I deserve that. I promise not to bother you again but I'm going to wait with you."

"Wait for what?" she asked suspiciously, releasing the door.

The phone rang as if on cue.

Victor pointed. "That should be Albright. A man has rung the hotel several times asking for you. Never leaves a message. Remember, let him do the talking."

She had been briefed, but as Andy went to answer the phone she felt as she had the first time she stepped on stage in a school play. She had been Cinderella in the sixth-grade production. She'd had to rush to the girls' rest room to throw up between each act. Right now, it felt as if the two grapes she had swallowed were tangoing on stiletto heels in her stomach.

"Hello. Oh, Les. Yes. No, of course not." From the corner of her eye she saw Victor streak across the carpet and scoop up the phone by her bed in the next room. "I was concerned, of course, when you didn't show at the cabstand. Oh, no need to explain. Of course I have your bag. I didn't know what else to do. Dinner? You don't need—but—well...when you put it that way, I don't suppose I can refuse. Fine. Seven o'clock. No, I'd prefer to meet you there. The Mansion on Turtle Creek. Sounds wonderful. See you there."

By the time she put the phone down, she almost felt sorry for Les Albright. Second thoughts began piling up like dirty socks on wash day. The man was allegedly involved in illegal activities, but the thought of being part of the trap to catch him made her stomach churn. She squelched the ugly memories that came to mind.

"You didn't follow instructions."

She looked up to see that Victor was once more in the room sporting the heaviest frown she'd seen on his face yet.

"What the hell did you think you were doing?"

She smirked. "Behaving naturally, as you ordered."

"You made a date with the guy." He sounded personally insulted.

Andy hunched her shoulders, annoyance curling inside her. "You said not to make him suspicious."

"I said—" Victor took a deep breath. "What is it? You couldn't pass up the opportunity for a free meal at the Mansion?"

"Underhanded tactics are your specialty, Agent Mondragon," she said nastily, "not mine."

His expression resolved into hard, uncompromising lines. "Don't confuse your players, Ms. Uchello. We're the good guys."

She scowled. "You couldn't prove it by me."

Victor stiffened like a soldier coming to attention, his voice holding a new and harder edge. "Albright's a criminal. Just because he doesn't commit his robberies with a Saturday night special doesn't make his actions any less illegal." He took a step toward her. "Two people died during the theft of the bonds and securities in that briefcase you picked up. The kind of merchandise Albright deals in often costs someone's life."

"Then why not arrest him?" she repeated for the second time this day, unwilling to concede him any points.

He shook his head as though she weren't paying attention. "Even if you testified against him, it wouldn't guarantee that he'd go to trial. He could claim you asked him to check the bag for you. His word against yours. On the other hand, there are those who might want to prevent you from testifying against him. The people who employ him aren't shopkeepers."

"You mean my life could be in danger?" Andy felt her skin ignite with the heat of fresh anger. "Why didn't you tell me this before?"

"I didn't want to frighten you," Victor said simply.

"And now?"

"I don't want you to misunderstand what's at stake."

"You might have made that more clear before he called." Andy tapped her foot impatiently as she gave the situation a little thought. "If I call back and cancel now, he'll want to know why." Hostility gave her dark eyes a brittle sheen. "I suppose I'm stuck."

"*We're* stuck," Victor amended, admiring the fact she hadn't lost her nerve at the idea she could be in danger. Guilt nagged at him as he watched her begin pacing the room in long, elegant strides. The last time he'd sent someone to tail Albright, an agent had ended up dead. He didn't want the responsibility of another death, especially a civilian's.

He glared at her when she stopped a few feet away. Her mouth was set in a sulky pout and the fragrance rising off her flushed skin quivered in his nostrils. His hands flexed into fists. He was angry and scared half out of his wits for her, but he couldn't let it interfere with business. "Get in and get out, tonight," he said in a deceptively calm voice. "Quick and clean."

Andy held his golden gaze several seconds, trying to read where the trap lay this time. But she saw only a cop's official concern, and something that seemed surprisingly like warmth. She looked away. "Right. In and out."

Feeling he had delivered enough tough talk for one day, Victor came slowly toward her. She looked tired but absurdly feminine with a trace of red lipstick smudged above the generous bow of her upper lip. Looking at it made him want to lick it away. And then linger to taste the rest of that softly fashioned mouth.

He touched her lightly, his large hands framing her shoulders with strength and determination. "I won't let anything happen to you. I promise."

Andy held still under his touch, willing herself to look up into his face and those intelligent eyes until she felt the full power of his confident persuasion. Too bad she didn't trust it. Too bad she couldn't trust him. "I believe you," she lied.

"Good." He dropped his hands from her shoulders as if touching her had been a reflex action, nothing personal. "I want you to do whatever it is you would've done if you hadn't been detained, only missed Albright at the airport. Act natural. Have dinner, hand over the case, and then get the hell out."

"My patriotic duty," Andy said, recalling his earlier words.

"Right."

She was surprised that he didn't smile again. Instead, he turned and walked away, his hands thrust into his trouser pockets. As he moved, the action molded the fabric to his taut buttocks. Whatever she thought of his methods of persuasion, she had to admit that Victor Mondragon had much to be proud of. Damn him!

VICTOR CAME SLOWLY to his feet as Andy entered her sitting room thirty minutes later. She was wearing a black dress—at least he supposed one called it a dress. To his eyes, she appeared to be wearing only a swath of see-through black lace.

After his mouth had gone dry with the mind-searing thought that he was staring at her thinly veiled skin, he realized that a layer of nude lining lay between him and wild fantasy. The bodice, a deep plunge into R-rated delirium, was held up by the tiniest straps he'd ever seen. The lace skirt hugged her sumptuously rounded hips before opening down the front at mid-thigh. Those long, long legs he had been admiring earlier were now encased in sheer black hose.

And her perfume! The elusive sensuality of eastern spices and floral notes made him want to bathe in it, if she would be there as his very own private bath toy.

There was no disguising his reaction. It was swift, sexual and blatant. If she cared to look, she would know she'd waved a red flag at one very touchy bull. "Why are you wearing that?"

Andy struck a pose. "What's wrong? Not patriotic enough for you?"

Victor opened his mouth then shut it. He was a professional. The least he could do was act like one. "You're supposed to be handing over a piece of luggage, not angling after that special someone." If the words weren't exactly detached, his tone of voice was.

Andy turned away from him and pretended to primp in the mirror nearby. She needed every ounce of confidence to pull off this evening. The dress, a designer original bought at seventy-five percent off list price, made her feel like a million. "You said I'm supposed to behave normally. When an attractive man asks me out, I make an effort to look my best."

"You've succeeded," Victor said sourly. Albright was going out with *his* fantasy. Somehow that seemed the final insult.

She turned back from the mirror, disappointed by his apparent lack of admiration. "Don't you have somewhere to be, like in the next room?"

Victor looked down and opened his hand. "There's just one more thing I need to do before you leave."

Andy's eyes narrowed suspiciously. She'd heard that tone of voice before—just before he delivered another rabbit punch. "What's that?"

He held up what looked like a hat pin. "Bug you."

"What, me wired for sound?"

"In stereo." Until she walked in, he had thought he would enjoy this excuse to touch her. Now he wished she was wearing jeans and a bulky sweater. The sacrifices he made in the name of duty. "Let's do it."

Andy lifted a single eyebrow. "You've got to be joking."

A brief smile traced his mouth. "You didn't think we were going to let you go it alone? I said I'd protect you." He slowly twirled the tiny microphone between thumb and forefinger as he came toward her. "This is your guarantee."

"There's no place to put it," she said briskly and started to turn away but he caught her lightly by one bare shoulder.

Looking down at her skimpy bodice he had to admit it presented a challenge. *And they said there were no frontiers left to conquer.* "No problem."

Andy watched in skepticism as he reached out very carefully and caught the low-cut line of her bodice just where it pressed against her cleavage. One long brown forefinger hooked into the black lace and tugged gently. Instead of making room for him to insert the microphone, his tug only allowed her breasts to swell more fully into the gap. She took an instinctive breath to keep from spilling out but the expansion of her rib cage tightened the material, trapping his finger in the pillowing warmth of her breast. Annoyed, she glanced up at him. The look in those tawny eyes regarding her was hot enough to melt premium-grade steel.

Victor wasn't certain when he stopped thinking rationally. Probably the moment his finger touched her unbelievably soft skin. Like a hound on point, he watched her bosom threaten to swell free as he tried to separate her bodice a fraction from her skin. Her fragrance was even more potent than the floral scent she had worn hours earlier. There were pungent base notes of exotic oils and the heady spice of rare woods. The scent scored through his mind, making him think of quiet dark places and slow wet kisses.

His hand trembled as he tentatively spread his fingers until all were lightly resting on the swell of her left breast. Then with his free hand, he inserted the tiny microphone between the inside lining and his trapped finger.

"Mission completed."

Andy heard his voice as if from a long way off. Yet when he lifted his gaze from her bodice, she realized his mouth was only inches from hers. His breath, warm and moist, feathered across her face. Her gaze fastened on his lips, a shade rosier than his bronze skin and so well modeled the edges were distinctly formed. It seemed the most inviting mouth she had ever seen. Instinct told her he was going to kiss her. A heartbeat before his mouth descended on hers, she closed her eyes and waited.

The knock at her door sounded like an ax splitting dry timber.

She jumped, they bumped noses, and what might have been a revelation turned into the embarrassed realization that she had been about to kiss a man she didn't even like.

Andy tried to turn away but couldn't. She glanced down to find the length of his right forefinger still tucked in her bodice. "If you don't mind." Unfortunately, her attempt at sarcasm sounded more like a plea for mercy.

For a second longer he stared unsmiling at her, and then he unhooked his finger. As the air rushed in to fill the void, Andy suddenly felt cold, then hot, then cold again. And bereft, as if she'd leaned out too far to grab for the all-elusive brass ring and nearly plummeted instead into disaster.

The second knock sounded natural, though muffled by the sound of her heart beating in her ears. She turned toward it blindly.

"Who is it?" she called before putting her eye to the peephole.

"Les Albright," came the reply from the other side.

The answer brought an unpleasant expression to her face. What the devil was he doing here? She didn't like men who didn't wait to be invited. She'd make certain he never took such liberties with her prerogative again. She reached for the chain. Then reason reasserted itself. She couldn't read him the riot act. She had a job to do, and that meant being pleasant. She glanced back for reassurance to where Victor stood.

He was gone.

"Hi." Andy forced a small smile as Les Albright entered. He was dressed in a dark blue suit that contrasted well with his bright gold hair and dark gold tan. Strangely, he didn't look nearly as attractive to her now as he had on the plane. Maybe it was because she had a new perspective on him. Or maybe, she thought with a jolt of memory, it was because she had just been staring into golden eyes fringed in coal black lashes.

He stepped inside before pivoting and giving her a full-length going-over. "Wow!"

"I hope it's appropriate." She fingered one tiny shoulder strap. "I've never been to the Mansion."

"You'd look wonderful in any setting." His blue eyes widening with male appreciation were as flattering as Victor's words had been disapproving, yet his admiration left her unmoved.

She didn't object when he took her by the arm and steered her out of the way so that he could close the door. Nor did she protest when his hand remained confidently on her arm as he followed her into the room. He seemed very certain of his welcome. She wondered how pleased he'd be if he knew a federal agent was in the next room listening to every word they spoke. Annoyed to be reminded of the fact, she turned suddenly to confront him. Victor had said be natural. Well, she would.

"I wasn't expecting you."

Albright annoyed her further by not replying at once. Instead, she noticed him give the suite a thorough once-over, all the while trying to appear casual. He even took his time in turning to her as he said, "The more I thought about it, the less I liked the idea of a beautiful woman having to navigate the city by herself."

Andy met his smile with a cool gaze. "I travel quite often, Mr. Albright. I'm accustomed to getting around by myself."

He couldn't miss her implication and had the grace to look embarrassed. "My mistake." He half turned, as if to leave. "Shall I meet you at the Mansion?"

Andy shook her head, satisfied that she had made her point. "Since you're here, I'll just get your case and my wrap."

He gave her an extra warm smile. "Leave the case for now. I can pick it up later, after dinner."

In your dreams, Andy thought as she headed into her bedroom. He was about as subtle as a four-inch headline. Maybe she should have chosen a different dress, after all. No, she decided as she entered the bedroom. She had wanted to relieve him of any suspicion about her actions at the airport. The dress must have worked. He hadn't even asked her what happened, yet.

When a long shadow detached itself from the darkened interior of her bathroom, Andy almost jumped out of her skin. Yet even as Victor motioned to her she was moving toward him. He put a finger to her lips as she was about to speak and drew her into the darkness and closed the door.

Shut in gloom, Andy heard him fumble with the toilet handle and then heard the sound of flushing. A moment later hands reached out for her. Suddenly she was against him, folded in a gentle embrace that enveloped her in his heat. She could feel his breath in her hair. His heart beat against the bare skin of her upper breasts. Every point of contact brought her body vividly alive.

"Don't be a hero," he whispered in her ear. His breath feathered across her cheek like a warm caress. "And don't provoke him. Albright might look like just another overachieving yuppie, but he's trouble."

Andy felt his fingers whisk across the low point of her cleavage. "Remember." He touched the hidden mike. "You're not alone."

She reached up and encountered the hard plane of his silk-covered chest. "I—I'll be careful," she whispered.

"Careful," he repeated so softly it seemed only a rumble within the deep solid wall of his chest. Somehow the word carried a much more immediate warning than when she said it.

She dragged her fingers across the silk, wondering what the man beneath would feel like. And then she remembered. He was a government agent on a job. She was part of his assignment. After a good dinner at a superior restaurant and handing off a piece of luggage, she would return to her life and Victor Mondragon would disappear like yesterday's rain. If she was lucky.

She backed away and he let her go, his hands falling away from her shoulders. "See you later," she murmured as she reached behind her back for the doorknob.

"Take a wrap. It's going to rain," he whispered, amusement leavening his voice.

He hadn't felt a thing, Andy thought as she slipped back into the bedroom. She was trembling from the effects of being in his arms. But—damn him!—for all she could judge, he hadn't felt even one tiny jolt of desire.

On the other side of the bathroom door, Victor stood in the darkness, grim-faced and breathing hard. It had been years since he had felt like a sweaty-palmed, sex-crazed juvenile. Touching Andrea Uchello had been a mistake. Playing eavesdropper on her date wasn't going to help things. Until she was again standing before him, her expressive dark eyes tangling gazes with his, he wouldn't take a single easy breath.

He tried not to think about the other reason his gut was churning like a cement mixer. But he could not *not* think about it. The first time he'd sent someone to deal with Albright, an experienced agent had turned up dead on a beach in Grand Cayman. Now he was sending a civilian to face the man. The necessity enraged and frightened him.

Victor bit off a curse as his hand went automatically to the pocket where he'd once carried his cigarettes and found it empty. It was going to be a long night.

Chapter Four

"You must be awfully well insured or so important you don't have to worry about losing your papers."

Les Albright looked up from his perusal of the Mansion's leather-bound wine list. "What papers?"

Andy sipped her aperitif before replying. He had just explained that the reason he'd not met her at the airport baggage carousel was because a business emergency had kept him on the phone nearly an hour. When he had finally finished, she was gone. Even without the certain knowledge that he was lying, his story would have sounded fishy. Victor had warned her to be natural, so she was naturally curious.

For not one second had she forgotten the device stuck inside her bodice. It was all she could do to keep from glancing down to make certain it was not peeking over the edge of her neckline. She hoped Victor and his friends could hear every word. Before this meal was over she meant for them to learn, from Albright's own lips, that she was a completely innocent party.

She smiled brightly at Albright. "I assume you must carry something important in a locked bag."

He pointed to a line on the list and then handed it to the waiting wine steward. Only then did he look directly at her. "Did you try to open it?"

"Why on earth would I? Besides, magnetized locks are impossible to open. Those things would defeat the average locksmith."

His brows lifted. "How do you know that?"

Andy swirled the lemon slice in her cocktail with a forefinger. Victor had told her after they had verified the contents, but she had a different answer. "In my line of business, it pays to know these things."

"Really?" His interest quickened. "Now that I think of it, you never once said during the flight what you do for a living."

"Neither did you," she responded easily. "I have a rule about never discussing my work while on the job. I'm a courier." She saw his eyes narrow and pretended to mistake the source of his scrutiny. "Surely you know what that is? I'm hired to carry things for people. Kind of like special delivery, only the deliverer is part of the package."

"I know what a courier is." His voice was cool and smooth as glass. "Whom do you work for?"

"Zane Couriers. It's based here in Dallas."

"Oh?" His expression lost all warmth, as if struck by a sudden chill at the mention of the courier agency. Strange, she thought, how easily he had hidden that icy veneer while aboard the plane.

"I've been with them nearly three years," Andy continued as if she didn't feel the hostility wafting off him like an Arctic wind. "Usually I deliver door-to-door. Other times I escort legal documents or business contracts from one city to another. Only rarely do I get the really fun jobs."

She had his full attention now and it wasn't hard to believe Victor's warning that Albright was a dangerous man. "What constitutes fun for a woman like you?"

"Are you really curious?"

"Absolutely."

Andy smiled but her cheeks were tight from tension. "There was the time a Dallas socialite flew to London with her husband for some big bash, the Ascot Races, if I remember correctly. Anyway, she had forgotten and left her jewelry case on her bed. Now, honey," she continued, mimicking the sugarcoated drawl of the lady in question, "ya'll just know she couldn't do without her favorite diamonds and pearls for some lil' old duke's ball." She paused to smile wryly at him. "So the company put me and the baubles on a plane and whisked us off to Merry Old England. My first time abroad, thanks to a rich woman's forgetfulness."

He smiled and seemed to relax. "Tell me more."

She did just that. She chatted through the salad and the main course, regaling him with stories of her very modest adventures as a courier. Her conversation would save the T-boys hours of research into her background, she thought tartly.

"Now that I've talked all through the meal," she said when their plates were removed, "why don't you tell me what you do for a living during dessert."

"It's really an amazing coincidence," he said slowly and met her look of inquiry with a teasing smile. "I'm a courier, too."

"Oh, right."

"No, really." As she continued to regard him skeptically, he leaned forward on his forearms. "You said yourself you never discuss your job while working. Neither do I. I specialize in valuable documents. Securities, bonds, things like that."

"Then why on earth did you check the bag? What if it had gotten lost or been stolen?"

He shrugged. "You'd be amazed how seldom a bag goes missing. I've lost more things in a taxi than by checking baggage."

Andy shook her head in mock amazement as she decided that his method of checking the illegal goods saved him from being asked to open his briefcase at an airport security checkpoint. It would be hard to explain bundles of cash, or drugs. Yet she knew she shouldn't exhibit any interest in what he carried.

"I almost never get to do anything exciting," she said wistfully. "I was once manacled with plastic cuffs to a valise. Airport security had a fit. Luckily, I had a police escort."

The waiter, who had just arrived with their desserts, gave her a very odd look as he set two chocolate soufflés down before them. She and Albright exchanged amused glances as the young man spooned Grand Marnier sauce into the desserts.

"Plastic cuffs?" he said when they were once again alone. "What the devil were you carrying?"

She chuckled. "You wouldn't believe me if I told you."

"Try me."

"They were reported to be the original plates for a soon-to-be-released nude photo spread of a rock star. The security precautions were purely for media hype, of course."

He grinned, thawing a fraction. "Were they raunchy?"

"Tastefully raunchy, I'm told."

"Of course."

She paused to taste a small spoonful of her soufflé. Then, as he did likewise, she said, "Does it pay well?"

He looked up from his soufflé. "What?"

"Your work. A courier like me doesn't make much."

He glanced pointedly at her designer dress. "You don't appear to be roughing it."

She shrugged. "Where there's a will there's a way. You ever hear of Hillsboro or San Marcus? They're a bargain lover's paradise. Acres of wholesale designer outlet stores, three and five hours, respectively, from Dallas."

He looked amazed. "Isn't that the middle of nowhere?"

She met his gaze squarely. "When you want something badly enough, you'll go the distance."

"And you're the kind of woman who, when she wants something badly enough, will go the distance for it." He licked his spoon. "Interesting."

Andy knew she should back away now. She'd played with fire long enough. Surely Agent Mondragon must be convinced that she was innocent of any wrongdoing. Yet, despite the voice of reason that sounded amazingly like Mondragon telling her to get "in and out," she was curious to know just how far Albright would string her along.

She reached out and lightly touched his sleeve, drawing his attention to her. "When I say I don't mind going after something I want, that doesn't mean I don't have scruples. There are things I won't do."

An unsettling warmth came back into his expression. "Such as?"

"Well, I wouldn't rob or shoot someone." She removed her hand from his sleeve. "And I won't sell my body."

He chuckled. "I really can't think of an instance where you'd be asked to do any of the above. Though, there are men who'd gladly pay a small fortune to spend an evening in your company. Just to have dinner."

Andy leaned slightly back from the table and recrossed her legs. "I know you meant that as a compliment but I prefer to choose my dinner companions without financial consideration."

"I definitely consider *that* a compliment." He lifted his brandy snifter. "To a beauty with a mind of her own."

Andy received his toast with a gracious nod but she was sorry she'd brought up the subject. The smarmy smile lingering on his mouth meant that the evening was likely to end in a tug of wills, at the very least.

He set his glass aside and, for several seconds, just gazed at her while Andy endured the uneasy feeling that she had somehow given herself away. Finally, he spoke. "What would you say if I told you I knew a way to increase your income without any risk?"

Andy carefully put down her spoon. Mondragon must hear her heart doing drumrolls. She mustn't blow it. Mustn't overreact. "I'm all ears."

A brief smile sketched his mouth. "It might trouble a few of your scruples."

Andy's personal anxiety meter went off the scale. "You mean something illegal?" she said softly, feeling justified in her nervous blink.

"Let's say my proposal falls in the area of sensitive issues." He leaned forward and once more rested his elbows on the table. She noted for the first time the tiny nick on his chin. Had he cut himself because he'd been preoccupied with thoughts of how to handle her? "Still interested?"

Andy didn't have to fake the quaver in her voice. "I don't want any part of drug dealing."

"Good lord! It's nothing like that." He reached for her hand, which lay beside her coffee cup, and gave it a squeeze. "I'm talking about temporarily detouring certain sensitive business matters, financial statements, or projected revenues—things a competitor would pay well to get a glimpse of."

Andy's eyes were wide open. "Isn't that illegal?"

He shrugged. "Industrial espionage goes on all the time. Whom does it hurt, really? Do you own major stock in any Fortune 500 company? High financiers live to gamble. You only have to glance at a newspaper to know they often cheat. Win or lose they're always back to play another day. A courier is just a messenger. If you get paid well to spend a few extra minutes in an airport while files are copied, isn't it worth a small risk?"

Andy was impressed. Not because she was in the least tempted by his logic but because she could see how easily someone who wanted desperately to believe him might be taken in. "I'd have to think about it."

"Of course." He released her hand. "I don't guarantee I could throw any business your way, even if you said yes. There'd have to be a background check." He smiled confidentially. "Do you have any serious indiscretions in your past you'd like to confess?"

"Oh, you mean the armed robbery I was arrested for at fifteen?" she questioned boldly. Too late she remembered that she wore a wire, and that Mondragon had no sense of humor that she could detect so far. Maybe she'd just bought the trouble she'd been trying to prevent.

Albright took it for the joke it was meant to be. "Seriously, you don't regularly bounce checks, do you?"

Andy almost laughed in his face. Here he sat offering to cut her in on an illegal courier racket, but only if she didn't cheat on her bank account. "I'll think about it. Maybe."

They finished their dessert in silence. He seemed suddenly preoccupied with his own thoughts while she couldn't wait for the meal to be over.

During the ride back in the cab he tried to kiss her. She evaded him and he simply moved a little away, as though it had been no more than what he had thought she would expect.

When she reached her hotel room, she turned before putting the key in the lock. "I'd ask you in but I'm really tired." She smiled. "Dinner was wonderful."

His eyes narrowed and she knew that he was debating the odds of overcoming her reluctance to continue the evening. Something decided him on the path of least resistance. "Of course. If you'll just fetch my bag."

The word *fetch* echoed in her head as she opened the door. Dogs fetched for their masters. It was a subtle insult but an effective one. He really was a nasty customer. No more chitchat with strangers. The next time she took a plane trip, she'd pack an interesting book.

She found the case where she'd left it by her bed. She noted in passing that the sheets had been turned back and a chocolate mint placed on the pillow. Exhaustion washed over her and she briefly shut her eyes. She couldn't wait to dive beneath those inviting covers. Forget breakfast. She'd sleep late and order room service for lunch.

Once back in the main room she moved briskly to where Albright stood and offered him the case. "Here you go."

His gaze moved slowly over her. "Sure you wouldn't like to share a brandy?"

"I'd fall asleep on your shoulder," she assured him.

"Sounds cozy."

She checked her inclination to smile. She'd been as nice as she was going to be. "Another time, perhaps."

He took the case and after a curt good-night, left her quickly.

As she turned away from bolting the door, the sound of applause didn't even startle her. She had assumed that Victor Mondragon was lurking somewhere nearby.

"'There are things I won't do,'" he mimicked from his doorway. "'I won't sell my body.' *Jeez!*"

"Oh, go away!" Blushing furiously, Andy reached inside her bodice to dislodge the microphone.

"No, please. Don't be modest." He stopped to pluck a grape from her arrangement and eat it as he sauntered into the room. "It was quite a performance. I especially like the way you circumvented his speculation that you might accept money to bed him. How did you phrase it? 'I prefer to choose my dinner companions without financial considerations.' Now that was class."

Andy hunched her shoulders against his scathing tone. "Don't you have some criminal to chase, some stolen bonds to sniff out?"

When his gaze met hers there was no amusement in his expression. He was furious. "What happened to 'in and out,' Ms. Uchello? I've seen children who didn't understand that fire is hot and professionals who lost it the first time the going got rough. But, lady, you're in a class all by yourself."

"I don't consider that a compliment."

"It's not."

He came toward her swiftly, long legs carrying him in purposeful strides that ate up the distance between them. She saw the warning glint in his golden eyes but she was too exhausted from the accumulated effects of the bruising day to rally for yet another battle. What could he do, she thought, besides yell?

He was breathing hard as he caught her by the upper arms. "Are you nuts! What the hell did you think you were doing?"

"Helping you," she answered in an angry breath.

His eyes dilated, the black eating up the gold. "You really want to help me? I'll show you how."

His mouth came down hard on hers.

The moment their lips met, Andy knew that this was what she had been waiting for all evening. For hours she had felt battered and bewildered by circumstances beyond her control. Yet, as she and Victor Mondragon had tangled and danced around each other like adversaries, she had grown ever more confused by her feelings. The signals were mixed, her emotions running in contrary directions. Now the reason behind her conflict became clear in the taste of his kiss.

It was so simple—it all came down to desire. He wanted her. She wanted him.

After the first bruising contact, his touch gentled. He turned his head, slanting the full length of his mouth over hers, and plunged the warm, wet muscular length of his tongue between her lips. Andy tasted raw need and the tart sweetness of fresh grape juice. An answering hunger rose up within her, along with the urge to understand, to explore this new side of the man who had seemed so perfectly in control.

He wasn't in control now. She felt the tension coursing through him. In the rapid heartbeat tattooing her chest. In the grip of his fingers flexed painfully on her arms. Victor Mondragon had lost his cool, and the result was a revelation.

His hands slid down over her body from shoulders to hips, cupping and holding and molding her to fit every contour of his. Her breasts spread across the hard planes of his chest. Her back arched, her midriff meeting washboard muscle. Where their hips met, the hard pressure of his sex dug into black lace, impressing upon her thinly clad body the heat and heaviness of his need. The rhythm of his forays into her mouth became quicker and more urgent. Again and again he entered and retreated, making love to her with his tongue.

Recklessly, Andy began pulling at his shirt, dragging the tail up out of his waistband so that she could find and touch him. Once he was free of his shirt, her hands went exploring and were rewarded with the texture of heaving muscle and dense, slightly damp skin. He was hot and oh, so smooth, more supple than the finest Spanish leather. She heard his exhaled breath hiss softly between his teeth as she began kneading the broad expanse of his back.

She went with him as he waltzed them backward toward the sofa and then he was pulling her down with him until they both sprawled on its cushions. She touched the hard planes of his chest as he slid one thin strap down her arm and then pressed a fiery kiss in the juncture between her shoulder and neck. Then he bent lower, catching the edge of black lace in his teeth. She squirmed beneath him as he tugged at the lace until the full glory of one of her breasts was exposed. His breath fanned the dusky nipple. It budded so quickly and so hard that Andy felt the tension deep in her womb.

He dragged his hot open mouth across her soft skin, as if needing to taste her. When he reached the crest his tongue began teasing it, lathing the nipple with the edge until she began to moan and move restlessly beneath him. When he took it in his mouth all the feeling in her body became concentrated at this point of contact. His cheeks flexed, suckling her, and Andy wondered dazedly why she'd never felt like this before. She was soaring, rising higher and dipping lower through the currents of desire. He seemed to know where all her most sensitive nerve endings lay just beneath her delicate skin and how to vary the pressure until she was melting down deep.

She grabbed handfuls of his hair, her fingers tightening right next to his scalp. If she hurt him, he gave no sign of it. She had never known a man to be so hungry, so much in need. His body began a slow, hard pumping of hers. She sighed at the sheer pleasure of the contact through the barrier of their clothes.

Wanting to help increase that pleasure, she reached down toward his hip, searching for the taut curve of his buttock.

What she encountered instead was a hard metal barrel of steel. She jerked away with a cry as though it had bitten her.

Mired in the heavy smoke of desire, Victor was slow to understand the cause of her reaction. Then, like a switch being flipped inside his head, he knew.

He reached back and touched his weapon tucked in the waistband holster at the small of his back. With a whispered curse, he pulled it out and lay it on the carpet as far away from them as his arm could reach.

Andy turned her head and stared at the lump of metal on the pale gray pile, and thought about what it represented. She didn't know why she hadn't noticed it before. Surely it had been there, bumping against her palms as she worked to free his shirt from his trousers. Now it was out between them, an ugly brutal reminder of who he was, and why he was in her life. He was a lawman. A federal agent. What could she have been thinking of?

"Let me go."

She didn't have to say it twice. Victor had seen her face when she spied the gun. Her expression was worth a dozen choice words. She no longer wanted him, or anything to do with him. He had seen that look on a woman's face before, but it was still a kick in the gut. He levered up and away from her and the sofa, gaining his feet in one agile movement.

Andy's gaze followed the shape of his well-toned torso clothed in naturally golden brown skin. Her fingertips tingled. She had touched that skin, wanted in a secret, shameful way to go on touching it. She shifted her gaze upward a few inches. His hair had come loose from its neat ponytail, its heavy blue-black silkiness sifting across his face as he worked to refasten his belt buckle. She remembered the sensual feel of his hair brushing her cheek, stinging across her sensitive lips.

"I'm sorry," he said, his head down so that she couldn't see his expression. Looking up, he waved his hand before his eyes, as if trying to erase some unpleasant mental image. "I shouldn't have done that. Call it bad judgment. Sometimes these things happen."

"What things?" Andy demanded and sat up, feeling as if she'd been left dangling over the edge of a very high cliff.

"Indiscretions," he answered, looking pained beyond what the moment required. "I crossed the line."

Andy fought the push of nervous laughter as she hustled her strap back up her arm to her shoulder. He made it sound as if they were both sixteen and had been caught in the act by her parents. "It was only a few kisses."

"Only?" The raw look he sent her said he had wanted a great deal more. "Even that is a breach of ethics."

She stared at him, alert now that he was talking about something more than their lovemaking. "Whose ethics?"

"Mine. You're a suspect and I'm on duty."

"Suspect?" Andy felt as if she'd been slapped. Her face seemed to catch fire. "After what happened tonight you can still call me that?"

He nodded slowly. "Officially, that's still your status. It's my job to protect and secure you."

"I see." Desire drained out of her so quickly she shivered. "In other words, I'm still in your custody."

"Yeah."

The insult registered like a fist in the pit of her stomach. Her conscience added a few jabs of its own. How could she have been so mistaken, so *stupid?* Chagrin nettled her cheeks. "Is this your usual method of protecting suspects? Or were you just entertaining yourself?"

"I never—!" He shook his head like a bull who'd suddenly been stung on the ear by a fly. "It just happened."

"Did it?" She thought it was what they had both wanted. Now she understood that he saw it differently. He'd invaded her privacy in just about the most intimate way possible but he saw it only as a lapse in ethics. Now he was looking at her like a little boy caught with his hand in the cookie jar. Only she had no pity to spare him. She was the forbidden sweet he'd tried to steal. She felt cheap, used, betrayed.

Unable to look at him any longer, Andy glanced around until she spied his silk shirt spread provocatively across the arm of the sofa. Irrationally annoyed by the sight, she picked it up between two fingers as if it were a soiled rag and tossed it at him. "Just for the record, I went along for the ride because I was curious to know if you could live up to the promise of your fancy packaging."

She let her gaze drift slowly across the expanse of his naked torso as she searched for words that would make him feel as used as she did. "If tonight was a fair sample of your technique, you should go into the trade. You could make a mint entertaining bored, wealthy women."

After she disappeared into her bedroom, slamming the door after her, Victor stood with his hands braced on the sofa back, his head hanging forward between his shoulders. He closed his eyes and forced himself to breathe slowly. It seemed his body would never stop throbbing with aborted desire. The taste of her lingered in the back of his throat. Her sweet, slightly musky scent, a more powerful aphrodisiac than any man-made perfume, clung in his nostrils. She'd been ready for him! If he'd been any slower, she might have stripped off his trousers for him. But it had been wrong, every damned delicious moment of it.

"Madre de Dios!" he muttered, adding self-deprecations in Spanish as they came to mind.

He was sworn by an oath and sense of purpose to do his job professionally, ethically and thoroughly. Nothing in his manual of procedure specifically covered the likes of Andrea Uchello. He had never completely lost control with a woman before. But he hadn't been able to think with his brains since she had turned around and looked at him with that combination of fear and anger and tough vulnerability during her interrogation. He'd felt struck by lightning.

He coughed up a chuckle. His reputation as a tough, by-the-book stickler had just suffered a blow. He had always disdained those who took undue advantage of the authority and power derived from their badges. But it wasn't like that with Andy. It had been personal from the first. What he wanted from Andy Uchello, still wanted right this second, was against department ethics. It might even be against the law.

Chapter Five

"Absolutely not!" Victor leveled his index finger at her. "Your part in this is over. Done deal."

"I think you're being unreasonable," Andy shot back, cradling her coffee cup with both hands. "Dictatorial and obstinate. But why am I surprised? All lawmen are bullies."

Victor simply glared at Andy as the waitress came toward them with a fresh pot of coffee in her hand. He had used the phone to ask her to meet him for breakfast in the hotel café, as much to reestablish civility between them as to avoid dealing with her in the intimate setting of their shared suite. But the morning light and the friendly chatter of strangers at the other tables could not completely dispel the lingering effects of the night before.

Victor watched Andy as the waitress filled their cups. When they had met in the lobby she had answered his smile with an unfriendly stare and the flat observation that he looked as if he'd slept in his clothes. The night before never happened—that was her hidden message. It was back to business.

She seemed a picture of casual elegance in a thigh-high yellow linen skimmer that managed to make her appear both provocative and aloof. But he had spent hours observing her and knew she wasn't as poised as she seemed. Every damned curl might be in place but the death grip she maintained on her coffee cup was a better barometer of her state of mind. She was furious. Yet how could she expect him to welcome her offer to further involve herself in his case? He not only did not welcome it, he wasn't even going to consider it.

Aware of his scrutiny, Andy took a deliberate sip of her coffee. Her eyes felt as if they were filled with grit and her head throbbed dully from lack of sleep but she refused to let it show. Last night had been a mistake, a lapse into a bad habit of flirting with danger. Now, all her instincts and past experience told her to run fast and far from the attraction he presented. The only reason she had agreed to meet him was that, about dawn, she began to think about what had occurred *before* she set eyes on Agent Mondragon.

Les Albright had set her up! What had he seen in her expression or behavior that translated in his mind to "perfect patsy"? She thought she had banished that vulnerability years ago. Now it was back to haunt her. She wanted revenge. Outsmarting Albright at his game seemed a satisfactory way to regain her self-respect. It should also put to rest any lingering suspicions the Feds had about her honesty. Yet, Mondragon wasn't treating her offer seriously.

As the waitress moved away, Andy's and Victor's gazes met, locked and held for an instant. Victor felt the intense discomfort of their mutual embarrassment, yet he was a field veteran and what he felt and how he behaved were dictated by his brain through separate wiring. His voice was coolly impersonal as he said, "Where were we?"

Andy hesitated only a heartbeat before returning to the point of their contention. "I was offering to be your contact with Albright. As I said before, I'm perfect for the job. He practically recruited me at dinner. You heard him."

"That was purely self-serving." Victor shook his head at her obvious naiveté. "He was feeling you out, trying to determine if you suspected anything."

"I know that." Andy took a calming breath. "I've had experience in dealing with men like Albright."

Victor met her gaze with a look that could crack ice. "Yesterday your alibi rested on the fact you didn't recognize his modus operandi. Are you switching stories?"

The question had all the subtlety of a sledgehammer, Andy decided as her cheeks warmed with indignation. "All right. I made a mistake. But this time I already know the game."

Victor hunched his shoulders. No way would he allow a civilian, let alone a suspect, to get further embroiled in his investigation. He could have offered a dozen reasons why but he knew she would continue to counter each one. Instead, he chose the most effective argument in the world. "No."

Andy dropped all pretense at conciliation. "I suppose you think I'm too dumb to pull it off. Or is it you just want further excuses to dress above your paycheck?"

Annoyance burned through the veteran tarnish of his eyes, leaving them intensely bright. "This isn't a movie. There's no glamour, no script, no rules once you cross the line into undercover. You're out there on your own. When you get in trouble, and you will, you probably won't be anywhere near the backup you were expecting. There's just you, your wits and your will to survive.''

Andy regarded him impassively. She could tell him a thing or two about survival, if she dared. Yet she was more curious about the hint at his own experience in that speech. "You sound as though you've crossed that line often.''

Victor wondered if she meant his work as a federal agent . . . or was she remembering, as he was, what he had said to her the night before. "Sometimes a man finds himself way out of bounds before he knows it.'' He smiled for the first time. "Sometimes it seems worth it.''

Confounded by his sudden change of mood, Andy glanced down into her cup. She didn't want sexual magnetism with her morning coffee. Not when she was still trying desperately to shore up the weakness he'd found in her emotional barrier the night before. Something deep down told her the pull between them wasn't just heat and loneliness. But she didn't trust herself. Too often she'd been betrayed by her emotions. She didn't need any more scars.

"Albright used me," she said slowly, trying to let the truth speak for her as she stared into her coffee. "I want revenge, okay? You need someone inside the operation to collect information on how this illegal courier ring is run. If Albright calls me, I don't see why I can't at least show some interest. If things get rough, I can always tell him I've changed my mind.''

"Is it the money?''

Her head shot up and she saw official skepticism lurking in Victor's golden gaze. Then she remembered that, the night before, he had heard Albright offer her an opportunity to make easy money. So, that was it! Even now, he wasn't quite certain of her motives.

She tapped down a sudden spurt of hurt feelings and let the antagonism she'd felt for him the day before kick back into play. "Right. I forgot. I'm the lady with expensive tastes. If I'm thinking of risking my neck, it must be for the cash."

"Prove me wrong," Victor said slowly, deliberately lacing cynicism through his words. "Stay away from Albright." He saw anger pinch her mouth and barely restrained softening his stance.

"You know what your problem is?" Her tone was combative. "You and Albright have too much in common. You think everyone has a price." She rose to her feet. "I don't have to prove anything to you. The law says a person is innocent until proven guilty. Even I. Now, if that's all, I have to go to work." She didn't wait for him to reply but turned and walked out of the café.

Victor let her go because he had to. Later, when she had had a moment to think about it, she would realize that he'd manipulated her once again into doing what he wanted. And he wanted very badly for her to walk away from anything to do with Albright. Of course, it meant she walked away from him as well.

He watched her go, admiring the slim line of her back and the gentle sway of her hips. He knew he would be a long time forgetting her. He could still remember the exact taste and texture of her mouth, relive her hands sliding over his bare skin. The unconscious recall had him growing hot and heavy behind his trouser zipper. He looked away. The next time he felt near losing control while on duty, he'd take it to the gym.

From the corner of his eye, he saw Phil rise from his seat at a far table a discreet distance away, folding his newspaper as he came toward him.

"You kids patch things up?" Phil inquired.

Victor frowned. "What are you talking about?"

Phil slid into the chair Andy had vacated. "Just a word of advice. In future, turn off the recording equipment *before* you make love to the suspect."

"Damn it!"

Phil grinned. "I erased the extraneous parts before turning it in to the department."

Victor smiled in relief. "Thanks."

Phil nodded. "That was fast. And unlike you."

"Yeah." Victor didn't need Phil to tell him that he'd done and said many things in the last twenty-four hours that were out of character. He offered no excuses. He didn't believe in excuses. He didn't need letting off the hook. He'd transgressed of his own free will. *Reality, deal with it,* was his motto.

Just when he could least afford a personal life, Andrea Uchello had walked through the door. Something about the way she affected him hinted that he just might have found the woman he had been looking for for a long time. Trouble was, he couldn't have her. He didn't have time to figure out the enigma that was Andrea Uchello and in his line of work he couldn't afford to be wrong about her. She had more spines than a cactus and a chip on her shoulder the size of a city block. It didn't take any psychological training to figure out she'd taken some hard knocks in life. Perhaps that's why she had kept her head during his interrogation yesterday.

He'd grilled enough suspects to know when one was hiding something. Andrea Uchello had been hiding something, something that made her dark eyes lairs where fear and wariness lurked. The trouble was, the secrets weren't necessarily related to his case. Had she been trying the night before to distract him from digging after those secrets? Or had she been as swamped by sensation as he?

His interest in her didn't prevent him from suspecting her motives. Some things just didn't add up. There was a gulf between her in-your-face attitude and the naked hurt he had glimpsed in her eyes the night before. She had been more than insulted by his rebuff of her. She had been momentarily shattered. Was what they had felt real, or an illusion?

"The necessary paperwork's been done," Phil said as the silence stretched out. "Ms. Uchello's lawyer is being notified this morning. She's free. So, what next?"

Victor squared his shoulders. "We go on."

"And Ms. Uchello?" Phil ventured.

Victor's eyes shuttered over. "History."

ANDY EYED HER COMPUTER screen in irritation. While she had been out of town some joker had replaced her old screen saver with one showing raunchy poses of a studly pinup in a G-string. The last thing she needed was a reminder of how good a well-toned male body looked stripped down.

"You get paid for ogling that man, girlfriend?"

Andy looked up over the half wall of her cubical into Keisha Jackson's cynical gaze. Between runs, Andy worked for Zane Couriers as a data entry operator. Keisha was her manager. "Practical joke," Andy answered and punched the escape key.

"Didn't look practical to me," Keisha replied, peering over the tops of her semicircular tortoiseshell reading glasses. "Personally, I prefer a man who looks like he spends less time at the beauty salon than I do." Expending a deep throaty chuckle her gaze moved from the video monitor to the framed picture beside it. "Now, that was a good-looking man." Her brows contracted together. "You still miss him, don't you?"

Andy turned her head toward the picture. The silver-framed photo was so much a part of her surroundings that most often she didn't notice it. It was a picture of Eric Connors and herself. It had been taken over a year ago at a Mardi Gras party. She had been high on Hurricanes and he on absinthe, the preferred drink, he assured her, of the most decadent of New Orleans's legendary characters. Eric looked great as always, a thick shock of chestnut hair brushing his tanned brow. He could have been a model with his clean-cut features and long, slim body. He had flair, he had style, he had big dreams and bigger ambition. He knew how to bend rules and make dreams come true. He was destined for big things . . . if he had lived long enough.

"Doesn't seem possible it's been seven months since his car went into Lake Ray Hubbard. You ever hear anything?"

"Not yet." Andy didn't like talking about the bizarre loose ends of Eric's death. "The police said it could be months before his body surfaced."

"Just as long as you're not waiting for him."

Andy heard in Keisha's tone a question that was confirmed when she glanced up and saw her manager's brows had formed a line of concern above her dark eyes. It was useless to pretend she didn't still feel the void Eric's death had left, but she had never found it easy to discuss her feelings. "I miss him and I wish his body would be found. But it's not as if we were into anything permanent."

"Good. He wasn't the sort of man for a woman to pin any dreams on." Keisha's bracing honesty cut across the sympathy in her expression. "A good time, all right, but flighty."

Keisha's blunt opinions seldom rubbed Andy the wrong way. She was the unofficial mother hen of many of the staff at Zane Couriers. She was married and had three children—in a word, stable. Like any good mother, Keisha could ferret out trouble no one thought to look for. But Eric was a very touchy subject, even with Keisha.

"Eric did a lot for me, more than you or anyone knows."

Keisha gave her a long, considering look over the top of her frames. "Do you know his mother's name?"

Andy frowned. "What?"

"I say, do you know his mother's name. Because I don't." She pointed to the picture. "Eric worked here four years. Two before you came. In that time, I never heard him mention his mother, or even if he had a family. Nobody even knew his real birth date because he kept changing it. The police investigation into his death put us on to the fact that his records with us had all been falsified. Eric wasn't even his real name." She bent a keen stare on Andy. "Don't you find that peculiar?"

"Things like birth dates and family connections weren't important to Eric," Andy offered in defense. The discovery that Eric had doctored his records had given her a few sleepless nights. Her own life was far from an open book.

Keisha nodded her head. "Like I said, flighty."

Andy shifted away from her manager. "Love to talk more but I've got work to do."

Keisha didn't move. She hovered like a vulture above the half wall of Andy's work space. Finally she said, "Have you worked out in your mind how it was that Eric died in an auto accident in Dallas when he told you he'd be out of town?"

Andy shrugged, not wanting any of her old anxieties or doubts raked up. "Eric didn't like anyone keeping tabs on him."

"Didn't you ever ask yourself why?"

Andy's head shot up. "What's the point now?" she asked with a hint of anger.

Keisha looked at her with all the objective sympathy of a physician about to impart bad news. "You're not nearly as tough as you'd like to think. A little truth might help you get on with your life."

Andy shook her head firmly. "I don't think I want to hear this."

"Too bad." Keisha moved into the tiny cubicle so that she would not be overheard by the other staff members. "Eric was in town that night because he'd specifically asked for the weekend off." Her voice dropped to a whisper. "He was coming back to town by way of Lake Ray Hubbard because of a certain woman who lives in Rockwall."

Andy resisted the urge to be insulting. "I've heard all the rumors about Eric sleeping around. People always gossip when they're jealous."

"I'm not gossiping," Keisha returned with a steady look that forced Andy to listen. "I'm saying it. Eric was seeing Marcie Jones from accounting. She gave notice the day after he died then claimed she was sick the next two weeks."

Andy's expression didn't alter though she felt suddenly chilled. "I heard Marcie left because she had a better offer."

Keisha smirked. "What she had was a guilty conscience."

"How do you know?"

Keisha compressed her lips, as if she were reevaluating the wisdom of her revelation. Then she said abruptly, "She told me when I threatened to hold up her final paycheck because of her absences. Said she couldn't face you after Eric's death—especially since he'd spent the last night of his life in her arms."

The news hit Andy broadside. *Eric had cheated on her.* Though she somehow wasn't surprised by the news, it still hurt, more than she expected. Nevertheless, she wasn't going to share that pain with anyone. "Is that all?" she said ungraciously.

Keisha's gaze softened. "I didn't mean to tell you all this, but you're holding on way too long to fairy tales. Eric was out for himself in the worst way. He didn't do you any favors you didn't repay, whether you realize that or not."

She tapped the frame with her pencil point. "You need to get on with your life, stop being Eric's widow." A smile softened her harsh words. "You're going to do better any day now."

Grim-faced, Andy lifted the silver frame from her desk and bent over to drop it into her leather back-pack beneath her chair. "So, what's on line for the week?" she asked in a normal tone of voice when she had straightened up.

A big smile of relief ripened on Keisha's mouth. "Mr. Zane will be in later in the week."

Andy's positive outlook dimmed a bit. "Why?"

Keisha chuckled. "Because it's his company."

"I hope it's on Thursday. I have a trip to Seattle on Thursday."

"Are you saying you don't like the man?" Andy saw Keisha's gaze sweep over her, taking in her sleeveless skimmer with its short hem. "He sure likes you."

Andy grimaced. "Trouble like that I don't need."

"Then you'd better hustle down to the feed store after work to buy a gunnysack," Keisha suggested wryly. "'Cause, girlfriend, in that outfit, you're advertising what's not for sale."

Andy laughed as she tugged at her short hemline, forgetting their harsh exchange of moments earlier. "Right. Ankle-length dresses and Doc Martens the rest of the week."

As her boss moved away, Andy turned back to her computer but she didn't immediately begin updating accounts. The week had begun abysmally and an appearance by Elijah Zane wasn't going to improve it.

In Texas, the name Zane was synonymous with money. If there was big money to be made, the Zane family usually had a cut of it. Oil, gas, real estate, cattle, even several of the new vineyards springing up in the hill country—they all had Zane money greasing their way. They risked big money like old-fashioned wildcatters and riverboat gamblers. Why the Zane dynasty's eldest son, Elijah Zane, hung on to a small if successful courier service was anyone's guess. Perhaps it was as Eric liked to say—"A man with Zane bucks can afford to scratch any and every itch!"

Andy frowned at her blank screen. Eric had offered the remark with great admiration, but she didn't think of it as a compliment. Some itches didn't deserve scratching.

Leaning over, she removed the frame from her backpack and touched the glass, tracing the outline of Eric's face with her fingertip as a sad smile tugged at the corners of her mouth. *Eric's widow.* Is that how her colleagues thought of her? Is that how she thought of herself? No, she and Eric had never planned anything permanent. He had his vices, as Keisha had pointed out. He liked to spend money he didn't have. And he didn't always tell the truth. She could picture his cocky smile as he said, "Truth's boring, Andy, something the dull and stupid cling to for lack of imagination."

Yet he had made her believe she could shed her troubled past like a snake sheds an old skin. He had given her a sense of self-worth she had never before possessed. So what if he hadn't been faithful toward the end? She had suspected he'd been about to leave her. He had been hinting at big things to come. Though he wasn't the love of her life, a part of her would always love him.

Since Eric's death, there'd been no man in her life . . . until Victor Mondragon.

Andy's eyes glazed as her libido took charge of her memory. Never once had she reacted to Eric's touch as she had Victor's. She had lain awake for hours go-

ing over what had happened—*almost* happened between them. She was shocked that she had behaved so
irresponsibly with a man who had been a complete
stranger only hours before. Worse yet, she couldn't
think of one rational justification for her behavior.
She had tried. She tested out the excuse that he had
swamped her reason with desire, which was true, but
it was not the truth.

The man was hot! She'd heard other women say
similar things about other men but her limited sexual
experiences had convinced her that such talk was
merely wishful thinking. Except, now she was thinking in those very terms. All Victor Mondragon had
had to do was kiss her and she'd all but ravished him.

Andy groaned and covered her face with one hand.
She hadn't known she could feel like that, wanting to
be the aggressor, to strip a man and make love to what
she found underneath. And she had been just getting
warmed up!

The content of her thoughts made Andy glance
furtively around between her splayed fingers. If his
gun, a symbol of the reason they were together, had
not interfered, she would have even more of which to
be ashamed.

On the heels of discomfort came a fresh spurt of
anger at herself. So what if she'd never before felt
anything remotely like that desperate attraction? Who
cared that thinking about him at this minute made her
toes curl inside her shoes? What had he called their
aborted seduction? An indiscretion. The word made
their actions seem inconsequential, like a thoughtless
remark. He couldn't possibly know how singular her
reaction to him had been. He couldn't guess, nor

would she have wanted him to, how much those torrid moments in his arms had meant to her.

Safe.

That's the word that had come circling back again and again in her thoughts during the night. Despite the attraction and the danger, she'd felt safe in the most risky embrace in town. Boy, could she pick them.

"Men!" she muttered as she shoved the picture back in her backpack and then bent over her keypad to begin making entries.

A few minutes later she heard a man say, "Ms. Uchello?"

Andy glanced up and her heart vaulted into her throat. "Mr. Lawson." Her gaze shot right past the lawyer into the hallway. "What brings you here?"

"A pleasant task, I assure you," Jim Lawson replied, sounding every inch an attorney on business. "It's my pleasure to inform you that all charges against you have been dropped."

Andy's gaze swerved right then left, snagging a pair of eyes peeping over the top of the half wall that separated hers from the next cubicle. She came to her feet. "Perhaps we should discuss this in private. I'm sure one of our conference rooms is open. Come with me." She deliberately leaned into the adjoining cubicle and said, "Would you mind covering my phone for a few minutes, Liz? Thanks."

Liz didn't even hesitate before saying, "What did you do?"

"I cursed out a cop who wrote me up for a rolling stop," she lied.

When they were safely behind closed doors, Jim offered Andy a copy of the statement she'd made to the authorities.

Andy scanned it, her eyes pausing a second on Victor Mondragon's bold signature, and then she looked up. "Now, tell me the truth? Will there be any repercussions from this? They can't change their minds tomorrow and reinstate the charge?"

"No." Jim smiled reassuringly. "They have no grounds to prosecute. I never really thought they did. They agreed that the whole thing was a mistake. You just happened to be in the wrong place at the wrong time. You can't be too careful these days. Need I say more?"

Andy shook her head, feeling her stomach unknot in queasy spasms. She knew she should leave well enough alone but she absolutely had to know. "Jim, remember when you asked me yesterday if there was something I wasn't telling you? Well, it has nothing to do with yesterday's events, but the reason I was so worried is that I got into trouble with the law once, years ago."

"Was it serious, Andy?" He sounded concerned but not alarmed.

"No, not exactly serious," she lied. This was ridiculous! She began pacing, wishing she could take back the beginning of her confession. "Something juvenile."

"Were you tried?"

She nodded, not looking at him.

"And convicted?"

This time her head barely moved.

"And you were afraid that if federal agents started digging into your background they'd come across this old file on you and be more inclined to believe you'd committed a second crime."

Andy darted a wary glance at him. "Exactly."

He smiled. "You needn't have worried. Juvenile files rarely interest the Feds, unless they're for a major crime like grand theft or murder."

"Oh, no! Nothing like that," Andy lied. "Driving drunk, underage."

"Well then, you were worried for nothing."

"I guess so," she answered, sounding less convincing than she'd hoped. She made herself smile. "Thanks. For everything. What do I owe you?"

Jim returned her smile. "Let's call it a professional courtesy call. I didn't want to lose my favorite courier." He patted her shoulder. "I'm glad you confided in me. Now that I know all the details, I understand your concerns, even if they were unwarranted."

Oh yes, he had all the details—except the real ones, Andy mused miserably once he'd left. "Like the fact it wasn't a juvenile crime," she murmured. She'd been eighteen. And it wasn't drunk driving but accessory to a robbery. And she hadn't gotten off with probation but rather six months in jail, commuted to two months in a women's detention center. *Then* four years probation. She'd bet a month's rent that information would have gotten Agent Mondragon's attention.

An hour later, Andy looked up as Keisha leaned once more over the partition into her cubicle. "I hear you got in trouble yesterday," Keisha said in her direct fashion. "Want to tell me about it?"

For an instant, Andy's heart stopped. When it began beating again, it was in slow hard strokes that shook her body with each pulse. Her chin went up, her eyes glaring a warning. "What trouble?"

Keisha cocked a brow at her. "Something about a traffic ticket?"

Andy hoped she didn't look as relieved as she felt. "The cop was rude," she said, damning Liz's gossipy nature and hoping a more elaborate lie wouldn't be necessary. "I responded in kind."

Keisha wagged her head. Her husband was a decorated police officer and she was loyal. "Girlfriend, the Dallas police don't play that. Next time, you call me and I'll see that Wendell takes care of things for you. Understand?"

Andy nodded, unwilling to offer thanks when it wasn't needed.

Yet as soon as Keisha walked away, Andy felt a stab of remorse. To block that feeling she bent over her computer and began pounding away on the keyboard. She wished she'd never met Les Albright. She wished Liz had minded her own business. But most of all, she wished she'd never set eyes on Victor Mondragon!

PHIL STOOD in the doorway of Victor's tiny office in the basement of Dallas's old federal building on Commerce Street. The building and its neighbor housed the city's federal offices, which put them in close proximity to the state attorney general. Because Victor and Phil were only temporarily assigned to Dallas, their accommodations were less than impressive. The work space was cramped and even with the air-conditioning doing its level best, the basement was stuffy. Both men worked in rolled up shirtsleeves and loosened ties. "Albright took an early-morning flight to Chicago," Phil said. "Do we proceed as usual?"

Victor nodded, looking up from the open folder in his lap. "The agents in Chicago know the drill. We're just going to have to wait for him to give us another opportunity to infiltrate. That could be tomorrow or next week." He dropped his feet, which he had propped up on the battered desk, to the floor as he swiveled his chair around. "That being the case, why don't you knock off and get some sleep? Last night was our third all-nighter in a row."

"I was hoping you'd say that. I have a date tonight." Phil shielded a large yawn with the manila file in his hand. "If I can keep my eyes open. Oh, by the way, here's Ms. Uchello's file, including the preliminary background check you ordered yesterday. Sorry it's late." He tossed the file on the top of the pile crowding Victor's desk. "There's nothing exceptional in there."

Victor scooped it up to shove back at Phil. "Then file it away."

Phil's expression was speculative as he accepted it. "Remember who you're talking to. Don't you even want her address? Phone number?"

"Don't need it," Victor murmured as chagrin wriggled beneath his calm surface. He didn't want her phone number because he didn't trust himself not to use it if he had it. The memory of her was imbedded in his mind like a sliver of glass—painful, sharp and bound to cause him more discomfort unless he could find a way to remove it. "I'm assigning her file to you. Should be easy work. Since her case has officially been closed, I doubt her name will come up again."

"If you say so," Phil replied. "Only, don't you think the cure is worse than the bite?"

Victor shifted in his chair, dodging images and remembered sensations stored in his mind from the night before. Yet he couldn't block out the aftermath, the raw anger in her dark eyes when he'd reminded her—

reminded them both—that theirs was an attraction that neither could afford to pursue. He felt a flush creep up his neck and hoped Phil didn't notice.

He was a professional. He couldn't allow personal desires to interfere with procedure. Until the Albright case was solved, she was still in his mind a quasi suspect. If necessary, Phil would handle her with the objectivity he couldn't seem to regain.

"Hey, Phil," Victor called as his partner turned to leave. "Why don't you see if your date has a friend."

Phil grinned and gave him the thumbs-up sign. "That's more like it."

Chapter Six

Andy stood with a fist on each hip as she considered the choices of clothing laid out on the bed. There was the black boxy jacket over which lay a gauzy print peasant skirt.

"Too hot," she murmured. It was, after all, August in Dallas. Next, a red formfitting sleeveless sheath screamed "look at me." Not good. The silk pantsuit, while one of her favorites, was also a no-no in the heat. The black cotton sundress sprigged with flowers was too informal. The navy shirtwaist with nautical piping was bound to draw barbed comments from Keisha.

Undecided, she turned toward the closet door, catching a reflection of herself in the full-length mirror hung there. She had tried on her first choice, a long natural linen vest, white T-shirt, and matching slim linen skirt that reached halfway down her calves. Eric had dubbed this her Miss Dowdy Does Dallas outfit. With a minimum of effort she knew she could turn it into something glamorous. Yet the point of the outfit was to make her seem less than scintillating. The staff had been informed last night that Elijah Zane would be in today, the day before she was to leave town.

"It makes a statement," she said to her image as she turned to make certain she was buttoned to knee level. "It says, thanks, but no thanks."

Zane had a reputation for laying hands on his possessions, as Keisha termed it behind his back. He wasn't a bottom pincher. He didn't need to be. His millions were as irresistible for some women as a Last Call Sale at Neiman Marcus. In fact, so many women were eager for his attention that she had escaped his notice, until Eric's death.

To her astonishment, Zane had dropped by her apartment a few days after the accident. With a basket of flowers in hand, he'd exuded a seemingly genuine concern over the loss of one of his employees. He had asked questions about Eric's family ties and then surprised her with the offer to pay for Eric's cremation—when the body was recovered. She had been relieved, for she couldn't afford the expense. Still, her natural suspicion had made her dubious of Zane's generosity. Maybe some people just had so much money that spending a few thousand on a near stranger didn't matter. Then an enormous floral bouquet had arrived the next day. After the third one arrived in a week, she had stopped accepting deliveries from the florist. She wasn't born yesterday, or even the day before. There were no innocent flirtations with a man like Zane.

During his subsequent visits to the courier office, Zane had never mentioned her refusal of his flowers. In fact, he acted as though nothing had ever occurred—and it hadn't. Yet she continued to be wary of his knowing smiles and lingering gazes. Maybe Keisha's casual observation was correct. There was no good way to discourage a man with an ego the size of

Zane's. He saw every woman's response to him, positive or otherwise, as a ploy to retain his interest.

A glance at her watch reminded Andy that she was going to be late unless she left pronto. She grabbed her things from the bed and thrust them onto the overcrowded rack in the closet. She had no room left for another single item, which meant she was going to have to clear out the front closet filled with Eric's clothing. She had kept them because she couldn't shake the feeling that once they were gone, so would all trace of the man who had been Eric Connors. As she hurried out the door, Andy recalled Keisha's advice. It was time to purge her life of memories.

Two hours later Elijah Zane made an appearance at the office. Entrance might have been more apt a term. There was drama inherent in everything Zane did. It was the details that gave his arrival the import of a ritual. As he walked through the main office, each member of the staff left his or her cubicle to greet him, forming an impromptu receiving line in order to shake the boss's hand. Afterward, everyone returned to work while Keisha followed him into his private office for a meeting.

Zane never came alone, and today two people flanked him, a young man in a pin-striped navy suit and a young woman in matching attire. However, she wore a skirt so short it didn't show beneath her jacket. Several men in the office did double takes just to make certain. But even a micromini couldn't shift focus for long from Zane himself.

Elijah Zane was in his midforties and weathering the years well. Tall and harshly handsome, he bore a marked resemblance to Clint Eastwood, sharing the same lean face, shock of dirty blond hair, wide slim-lipped mouth and steel gray gaze. He possessed the eager grin of a boy in a candy shop with all of his allowance gripped in his fist. With the glad-handedness of a politician, he shook hands and spread his benevolent smile around the office.

Andy deliberately hung back until she realized, too late, that by doing so she had allowed herself to be his last stop and thereby garnered his lingering attention.

"Hi there, Ms. Uchello," Zane said as he clasped her hand in his firm grip. Instead of letting her go, he added the pressure of his second hand as he leaned in toward her, his brows contracting in a frown. "What's this I hear about you getting into some trouble with the law earlier this week?"

Andy's pulse leaped so strongly she suspected he felt it, too. She had thought she had escaped! Why hadn't it occurred to her before that the Treasury Department wouldn't have gone to her manager but taken their suspicions straight to the owner? She could almost hear Victor Mondragon's blunt baritone offering facts that left plenty of room for innuendo. She had a top security clearance, which any whisper of misconduct might jeopardize.

Zane stood there, still clutching her hand during the awkward moment. Well, she had nothing to confess, if that was what he was waiting for. Anger at the unfairness of her situation snaked through her, snapping in her eyes like whip tails as she stared back at Zane.

He leaned in toward her again. "You've been fooling us all into thinking you were one cool customer. Now I know your naughty little secret."

Andy remained still when he reached up and placed a hand on her shoulder. She fought the impulse to ask him, beg him, to hear her side. "I don't know what you mean," she said abruptly.

"I mean, only a wildcat would take on one of Dallas's finest!"

While the others chuckled at her expense, including the two strangers with Zane, Andy struggled with an entirely new set of emotions. She knew she should feel relieved, but all she felt was the white-hot rage of resentment. That stupid if convenient lie about a traffic ticket would not die. Worse yet, Zane had used it to embarrass her. She didn't like bullies, whether they wore dusty Stetson hats and battered boots, like her father, or custom tailoring. "It wasn't a big deal," she said between barely unclenched teeth.

"You needn't explain, Ms. Uchello." Zane grinned as he patted her shoulder as if it were a dog's head. "But next time you get a ticket, you just phone me." He spared a glance for Keisha, who stood nearby. "We've got a few friends at traffic court. Isn't that right, Mrs. Jackson?"

"Ms. Uchello and I have discussed that," Keisha answered without cracking a smile.

Annoyance ricocheted through Andy's thoughts. Why was everyone so eager to "fix" her nonexistent traffic ticket? No sooner had the question formed than she saw the answer in Zane's gaze. A favor done was a favor owed. If he expected a thank you, he wasn't going to get it.

As the phone behind her rang, she turned her head and took a step backward, forcing him to release her. "Excuse me, I must take this call."

She almost got away.

"You doing the Seattle job tomorrow?"

Zane's inquiry brought Andy up short as the phone rang a third time. With a sinking feeling, she turned back to let her voice mail pick up. "Yes, sir."

He frowned at her. Andy knew he disliked being addressed as "sir." He preferred even employees to call him "Zane," saying that "sir" made him feel old. He was old enough to be *her* father. Her father. She dodged the thought. She had enough on her hands without dredging up specters from the past.

"We need to talk about that account, Ms. Uchello. Our customer is seeking a courier to fly a regular Tokyo route. Could become regular employment, for the right person."

His grin implied more than his words. She was going to have to deal with him today. But she didn't have to sound pleased. "I'm rather busy today. When would you like to discuss this, Mr. Zane?"

"Lunchtime will do," he said smoothly. "I've got to catch a plane for Houston at three o'clock. I suppose you're free at noon?"

Andy smiled. "If it's that important."

She saw his gaze sharpen as he digested the implication that she might have other plans she didn't want to alter. "Noon. At the Deep Ellum Café. I don't have much time to give this."

Good, Andy thought as she turned away again. Snagging a regular international route had been a dream of hers ever since she took this job. But she wasn't going to beg for it. Eric once said she had a chip the size of Texas Stadium on her shoulder. Over the years she had managed to whittle it down, but she hadn't lied to Albright when she told him there were things she wouldn't do for money. Getting into debt with Elijah Zane was one of them.

IT WAS NEARLY 9:00 p.m. and still ninety-five degrees when Andy pulled into her parking space at her apartment on Herschel Avenue. Unable to relax after work, she had gone to a movie and then treated herself to a little shopping. Eric had preferred to live close to downtown. Since they couldn't afford his dream of living on posh Turtle Creek, they'd rented space in a funkier neighborhood off Oak Lawn. The small two-story, 1920s-era brick apartment had the architectural feel of a prairie house with wide roof lines, brick facades and matching columned porches. She shared one four-apartment space with a hair salon and an art boutique, both downstairs, and a gay couple next door, who were never home much. Therefore most nights, after the businesses closed, they had been basically alone in the building, which had never bothered her while Eric was alive. But, lately, she had been thinking about finding a more neighborly place.

She climbed the stairs to the second floor with leaden steps. Zane had waved the Tokyo job under her nose during lunch. The courier would have to live in Seattle, he'd said. She'd admitted that she wouldn't mind starting over in a new place. Then he had made the mistake of dangling the possibility of his company picking up the moving expenses and temporarily boosting the courier's salary "to help with settling-in expenses." Suddenly there were so many strings attached that the job had taken on the appearance of a parade balloon. She had tried her best to remain noncommittal through the rest of the meal, then flown off like a canary who'd spied an open cage door. She had had the rest of the afternoon to think about why she'd panicked and passed up a perfectly good job offer.

Sometimes pride was a burden. At least the worst week in a long time was behind her.

Balancing her grocery sacks in one arm, Andy aimed her key at the lock. As she shoved it in, the door swung open. Dread raked up her spine even before she reached out and flipped the switch just inside the door.

She remembered fleetingly how she always booed louder than anyone else in the audience when a character in a horror movie walked into an obvious trap, like opening the door after the knob had been rattled from the outside or going down into the cellar after the lights had mysteriously refused to work. But she was drawn into the maelstrom by sheer disbelief. Her mind refused to accept the simple truth of what her eyes saw.

The pictures still hung on the wall, the antique mirror, even the silver candlesticks remained on the mantel. Surprisingly, even Eric's prized audio equipment remained untouched. Everything else in the room seemed to have been tossed by gigantic salad tongs. Sofa pillows lay scattered. Books toppled from shelves. Papers spilled from open drawers. Lamps had been upended onto the floor. End tables were pushed askew.

She wandered like a sleepwalker into her bedroom, knowing before she entered it what she would find. It was as if the room had exploded. Nothing was left untouched. The mattress had been upended against the headboard. The contents of her closet emptied. Thousands of dollars worth of clothing lay in twisted piles where they had been flung, hangers still attached. Bedding, belts, shoes and lingerie added to the confusion. Jewelry, dumped and sifted through, winked in the overhead light like a pasha's treasure horde. *Yet, it was all there.*

That phrase kept pumping through her stunned thoughts as she recrossed the hall into the living room in search of her phone. Why hadn't the intruders taken anything?

She was blindsided by the shove that sent her sprawling across the hardwood floor of her living room. She wasn't a screamer but the urge to imitate a horror movie heroine's piercing scream came quite naturally. Her cry was cut off by a knee landing in the middle of her back. The force of it expelled her breath in a painful explosion and then something hard, cold and metallic nudged her behind her right ear.

"Don't move! Stay down!"

The voice was a rough whisper. Male. Part of her mind booed her gullibility but the other, dominant part was reacting out of raw terror. She tried to draw breath so she could give that scream one more try. But the hand at the back of her head pressing her face onto the cool surface of the oak floor couldn't be ignored. Nor could the nature of the danger she was in. So damn stupid! She should have run while she had the chance. That seemed a pitifully inadequate last thought.

"NOW WHY AM I NOT surprised you're still here?"

Victor looked up from the reading he was hunched over. Phil lounged against the doorjamb looking as cool as a fresh head of lettuce. Victor was hot. Perspiration slicked his face. Sweat ran in trickles beneath his cotton dress shirt. His sleeves were rolled back and his tie hung in a limp knot against his half-unbuttoned shirtfront. Nothing helped. The building's ancient air-conditioning system had been out most of the day, forcing many federal employees, including Phil, to flee. But Victor had stayed because he was too wound up to take any pleasure in an excuse for time off. He was hot, tired, frustrated and ready to vent his anger.

"I've been going over Albright's file again, trying to anticipate his next move." He slammed his fist down on the paperwork. "We should have had the bastard. Should have nailed him!"

"I thought last night was supposed to take the edge off things."

Victor knew he was referring to the fact that after their double date, he'd offered to see his blind date home. "Nothing happened."

"Nothing?"

The look in Victor's eyes made Phil raise his hands in a gesture of surrender. "I have just one more thing to say." He pointed to the file Victor held. "When work gets personal, judgment gets screwed. We all took it hard when Randall bought it. I was in on the decision to send him in, too. It could have been any one of us. You'd better throttle back. Albright doesn't take chances. Odds are, he'll stay put for a while. When the time comes, you'll get another crack at him. Until then, you have to live. So, how about some dinner? *Chiles rellenos? Carne guisado? Shrimp empanadas?*"

Victor shook his head. The thought of food made his stomach crimp. "I'm busy." He glanced down. The gesture was clear. No company wanted.

From down the hall came the sound of a phone ringing. Victor glanced over in annoyance at the light flashing on his phone. "That's your line. Take it somewhere else, will you?"

Phil smiled at the blunt invitation to leave. "Back in a flash. I need a margarita in the worst way."

He was back in thirty seconds flat, his eyes bright with intrigue. "And they say there's no reward for the wicked. Let me make your day, boss. One of my contacts at the police department thought we might like to know about a 911 that came in just now."

Victor reached for the cup of coffee he'd just poured. "I'm sort of busy here, Phil. Do you have anything useful for me?"

"It was a break-in and assault at 4213 Herschel. That's Andrea Uchello's address."

Victor stood up so quickly he spilled coffee in his lap. "Who called it in?" he asked, adding a curse as he brushed at the damp spot on his slacks with his free hand.

"The resident."

Victor's head shot up. "Is she okay?"

"What's it worth to you?"

Victor released an impressive string of profanities that snapped Phil's head back. "Right, I'm jerking your chain. The dispatcher said she sounded shaken. She surprised the perp. But unharmed."

Victor forced his mind to consider the crime and not the woman. But his body wasn't listening. His heart was pumping adrenaline through his system. He felt ready to weight lift a Volkswagen. She had surprised the intruder. Sweet heaven! "Tell me that address again."

"It's 4213 Herschel."

Victor put his coffee cup down very carefully. His hand hardly shook at all as he reached for his pen and jotted down the numbers. When he was done he simply stared at what he'd written before lifting his head. "Why does that ring a bell?"

Phil summoned up a pretty good leer. "You tell me."

Victor's expression was minus all emotion but sincerity. "I know that address and I don't think it has anything to do with Ms. Uchello." He reached down and punched a few keys on his computer. Then he waited, watching the screen flicker until a list of names and addresses came up. "What the—" His expression darkened. "I think I'd better take a gander at Ms. Uchello's file, after all. Alert the police that we do want in on this but keep it quiet. Let me know minute by minute what they find."

"I'm way ahead of you. We're already hooked up." A doubtful look passed over Phil's face. "What did you find in the computer? I thought you were convinced she's clean."

"I said probably." Victor looked up from the screen. "The probabilities just altered. So, I'm taking the case back."

He could see Phil struggling with his curiosity. After all, he had given the Uchello file to Phil just two days ago. Now he was taking it back, no explanations offered. His eyes narrowed. "Did I forget to say please?"

Phil levered himself away from the doorjamb. "I'll get her file."

As soon as his partner was out of sight, Victor braced his arms on his desktop and lowered his head to take several long, slow breaths. His fatigue had caused him to overreact. Perhaps fatigue also explained his major blunder.

"Son of a—" he muttered and levered himself away from the desk. The monitor's pale eye stared him in the face with a fact he'd been too tired, or distracted, to notice before. He reached out and punched the power key. The monitor went dark.

He didn't want to say anything, even to Phil, until he had pieced it together in his own mind. If he was right, he was going to look very stupid in more eyes than his own. One thing was certain, Andrea Uchello had smoked his mind more than he had realized. What else would explain why he'd missed the connection?

Her address—4213 Herschel—was the same as that of another suspect. Victor bent and jerked open his drawer to extract a file on the late Eric Connors.

VICTOR STOOD more than a minute at the bottom of Andrea Uchello's stairwell, trying to decide on his tactics.

What he had discovered couldn't be ignored. His chagrin could be ignored, his sense of disappointment, too. Certainly his weariness and hunger could be subverted to feed his sense of justice and zeal for the truth. Even anger had its purpose. It put an edge on things, filtered out the subtleties, kept him focused. He had a feeling he was going to need all of the above to help him stay centered with Andrea Uchello in the same room. She'd played him like a fish and he'd swallowed her innocent routine, hook, line and sinker. That realization smarted.

He glanced at his watch. It was well past 11:00 p.m. He'd waited for the police to finish their investigation and clear out.

A habit borne of experience, he mentally cased the stairwell before starting his climb. He noted that a single short strip of yellow police tape lay trampled on the stairs. When he reached the top he noticed that there was no landing. The top step was on level with the door. A thief in a hurry might have misstepped and tumbled down the narrow, steep flight. That was the initial conjecture of the police to explain the smear of blood they had found on the wall near the bottom of the stairway.

Victor peered at the brownish smudge in the dim light. He had been told it was the intruder's. Unfortunately, it didn't contain any usable prints.

That telltale smear of blood was the only reason Victor was hesitating. The break-in was real. The reason for it remained to be explained. The police said nothing was taken. The incident might have been a prank except for the fact the victim was certain she had been threatened with a gun. That worried him because he couldn't afford to care about Andrea Uchello now.

Victor wanted her to be innocent, but wanting didn't make it so. If he went with his feelings again, he was going to regret it. The new information he had, the reason he was here, had nothing to do with the break-in.

He recalled another crime scene, in Grand Cayman, where there had been more blood and a body. The reason why he wanted Albright, wanted him so bad the taste of that wanting was like bile from an ulcer, realigned his concentration. It wasn't his battle alone. As Phil had said, it was personal, for his entire unit. But the responsibility was his. To do his job well he couldn't let anything, especially his feelings for Andrea Uchello, matter.

He pushed the doorbell and waited, guts as tense as guitar strings.

She came surprisingly quickly to her door. The hallway light went on over his head, a yellow bug bulb that turned his bronze skin the color of putty. He saw a shadow at the peephole, heard a dead bolt being drawn, and then the door swung wide.

"Victor!" The smile that lit up her face made him feel like the lowest kind of cheat because, before he left here, he intended to wring a confession out of her.

Chapter Seven

That brilliant smile lasted as long as it took her to remember who he was—what he was. He saw with real regret the warmth die in her dark eyes and the corners of her mouth straighten. She stepped into the space of the half-open door and braced her arm on the opposite side, physically negating the implicit welcome she had moments before offered. "Agent Mondragon, what are you doing here?"

Agent Mondragon. Victor knew he should flip out his badge, draw the line deeper in the sand, give her every chance to defend herself. She was going to need it. But he couldn't look away from the angry red bruise blossoming on the left side of her chin. The intruder had struck her! Bastard, he thought, cowardly bastard. "Are you all right?"

She nodded once. "I had a little set-to here a while ago. No big deal."

He was surprised to hear the western twang replace her usual carefully enunciated speech. It drew his attention to her faded jeans and the Dallas Cowboys T-shirt that had been cropped to her waist, its sleeves cut out. Her feet were bare and the ends of her hair were shiny and damp and clung in C-shaped hooks to her cheeks, as if she'd just stepped out of the shower. Without a trace of makeup she seemed younger, softer, more fragile. Yet there was nothing of the waif about her. Her nicely toned body seemed less about style than a reflection of the tense energy radiating from her. Everything about her cut across the aloof sophisticated image of the woman he had met three days ago. That bothered him even though he knew her edginess would make his job easier. For his own selfish peace of mind, he wanted to feel he was facing a worthy adversary. But he didn't touch his badge or tell her his purpose.

"What happened? Fight with the boyfriend?" he suggested, curious to know what she'd tell him, the truth or a lie.

He saw her fingers tighten on the edge of the door. "I was burglarized."

He didn't intend to do it but his hand was suddenly hovering at her jaw, his fingers framing but not quite touching her mistreated chin. "You were assaulted."

Her mouth quivered a moment. Her fingers raked down the side of the doorjamb, brushing his hand aside, and then she stepped back, dragging the door wider. "See for yourself."

He'd seen plenty of ransacked places. He'd even wrecked a few himself with search warrant in hand, looking for clues, for information, for stolen securities, counterfeiter's templates, drug money. It never ceased to amaze him how much damage could be done in so little time. He walked in slowly, aware that she remained by the door, as if ready to ask him to leave. Was she still angry over their last confrontation?

He didn't glance at her but allowed his mind to record the scene before him. She had been trying to clean up. The sofa pillows were all in place. One end table lamp was lit while the shards of its broken companion had been swept into a neat pile on the other side. Books and magazines had been stacked in columns before empty shelving. CD casings and a dozen other bits of bric-a-brac littered the floor. Clothing belched forth from the closet in the narrow front hall. Men's clothing.

Victor kicked the curled end of a throw rug flat. It didn't take much imagination to guess how horrible this must seem to her. Still, things could be replaced. If she'd been broken like the lamp, it would not have been so easy for him to dismiss.

He turned to where she stood by the door. It was closed, much like the expression on her face. "You were lucky."

"Lucky?" Her tone was incredulity wrapped around contempt. "The police said I'm lucky because I didn't lose anything that matters. What about the fact that I feel violated?"

Victor watched her rub her hands up and down her bare arms as if trying to erase a touch. The intruder's? His mind kicked back over the police report he'd scanned. Rape wasn't mentioned. But what wasn't in a report left a lot to the imagination. The bruise on her chin was quite real. She'd at least been manhandled. "Did he hurt you?"

"Not really." She shrugged, a defensive posture coming into play as she snapped out the words. "I surprised him. He surprised me. I've been roughed up before."

"When?"

Hostility leaped into her gaze. "As a kid. On the playground." She laughed. The sound was short, tough and too brittle to carry the beauty of her usual laughter. "I was a barrel-rider in my teens. You learn to take a spill at full gallop, swallow the grit in your teeth and come up smiling."

Victor ignored the bravado. Despite it, she looked thoroughly shaken, more so than when he had threatened to have her booked and jailed. He thought he understood why. A break-in was the closest thing to rape, an invasion by a hostile force into the private world of another person. Most people saw their belongings as an extension of themselves. Attack, violation, assault—victims of break-ins often expressed their feelings in terms of abuse.

Abuse. His mind caught and held on the word. "Did anyone ever hurt you before, Ms. Uchello?"

"Andy." Her mouth worked against the temptation to smile. "People call me Andy."

He heard the unspoken offer of friendship and it made him even more uncomfortable. He was here to question her, break her down—maybe ruin her life. Yet, he had been taught to use whatever manipulative tools a suspect offered. But he didn't like it. "Okay, Andy. So, who hurt you?"

She lifted her chin, dark eyes like train tunnels. "You want a listing by names, dates and relationships for your record? Or will a general survey do?"

"General will do," he replied, wondering bleakly how many names would be on that list. She looked as if a harsh word would break her, but her combative spirit was proof to the contrary.

She took a few steps toward him, as if to convey that she wasn't daunted by his presence. "Let me make this simple for you, in words of one syllable. All my life men have hurt me." Her expression made his hair stand on end.

"Abused?"

Her chin pulled in against the question but that did not stop her from replying. "Not in the legal sense. My dad didn't beat me." Something flashed in her eyes. "He wasn't around enough for it to come to that. I believe they call what he did benign neglect."

Suddenly she seemed to remember herself. The transformation was instant and miraculous. She straightened her spine, her expression reforming into the haughty composure she had shown the day they met. As she tucked a feathering of curls behind one ear he saw that she wore delicate pearl studs. He caught for the first time the subtle scent of her perfume and it drew him unwillingly into a memory of the feel of her soft skin beneath his lips. Wherever she had temporarily gone, the Andrea Uchello he had first met was back. Her next words confirmed as much.

"I discovered early in life that a woman can't be too nice or some man will mistake her niceness for weakness and use it against her." Her dark gaze found his, aimed carefully for his psyche and fired. "Haven't you found that's the way it works for you, Mr. Mondragon? With all that muscular attraction and menace, you must have sneaked under many a deluded woman's guard."

Victor smiled, inwardly saluting her ability to turn the tables on him. So, he was a big bad man, guilty by association in her mind with all the other men in her life who'd taken advantage. It was a good ploy. He'd never sold her short on brains or nerve. That understanding didn't stop his better nature from wanting to take up the challenge and prove her wrong. But his job demanded he act otherwise. He broke their visual contact. "Why would someone break in here?"

She gestured broadly with a hand. "Look around. There're plenty of things worth fencing."

Victor had noticed the quality pieces of audio equipment on the nearby shelves, CD player, tape deck, TV monitor, speakers. "So why didn't the intruder take anything?"

He saw her frown. "I don't know. Maybe I came home too soon."

"Or maybe it wasn't a robbery." He watched her face for any flicker of agitation that might tell him he was on the mark. "Maybe he was after something specific."

She looked up and again snagged his gaze in the net of her anger. "Like what?"

"You tell me."

Her smile played out slowly, knowingly. "Stolen securities, maybe?"

Victor hesitated. Had she guessed the reason behind his appearance, or was she just teasing him? Suddenly he felt a hundred years old. He was usually better at covering his tracks. Fatigue was costing him his edge. He glanced over at her sofa. "Do you mind?" he asked, moving toward its inviting softness before she'd given her consent.

Andy eyed him warily. Why was her heart pounding as she watched him cross her living room? She didn't want him here, didn't need him. Or, maybe that was it. She did want him to stay and the thought was scaring the hell out of her.

Using an old trick to boost her confidence, she concentrated on his flaws as he settled himself in the

downy contours of her floor-sample indigo silk sofa.
The flaws were numerous.

He did *not* resemble a fashion layout this night. The
navy blazer he wore was hopelessly out of date. His
rumpled shirt was wilted and splattered with coffee
stains. And his tie—well, it begged a pair of shears be
taken to it. Her gaze moved to his face. His tied-back
hair was mussed, as if a repeated impatient gesture had
raked it loose. Even the luster of his gorgeous face was
tarnished by parallel lines of weariness. He was no
glamorous bad boy Adonis this night. His aura of
danger had dimmed. Tonight he looked like what he
was, a weary man with an essentially dull, if occasionally dangerous, job.

But despite his fashion flaws, Victor Mondragon
was everything her catalog of dreams listed: tall, dark,
handsome—and something much more important. He
still projected a rock steadiness that had made her un-
reasonably happy to see him at her door tonight. Her
first impulse had been to launch herself into his arms.

She chided herself for the weakness even as the
feeling lingered. She told herself her neediness was
based on a purely emotional response to a familiar
face after enduring a hellish evening. So then why did
his presence make the barriers around her heart tremble like the walls of Jericho at the sound of a trum-
pet?

When he suddenly looked up at her she felt X-rayed,
her feelings exposed, and that scared her more than
the intruder with the gun. Wanting to distract his focus from her she said the first thing that came to mind.
"He stole a picture."

"I beg your pardon?"

His momentary discomposure pleased her. "The thief took a picture, a photo."

He hunched forward and she saw him reach toward his jacket pocket but at the last minute he aborted the gesture. "What of?"

"My boyfriend and me."

Incredulity eclipsed the weariness from his face as he chuckled. "You're kidding?"

Andy went over and picked up the silver frame on the mantel. "I didn't notice until after the police left. I thought at first the photo had fallen out. Then I noticed that the back had been pried open." She held it out for his inspection. "Sick, isn't it? Like the beginning of a stalker movie."

Victor noted the weight of the heavy silver frame and surmised the picture had been valuable to her. That meant the boyfriend's memory was valuable. But just how valuable? Enough to lie for? To cheat for? Discipline told him to take his time, come back to that issue later. Right now he would follow her lead, see where she wanted to take him. "Do you have any reason to think you're being stalked?"

Andy sank onto the tasseled hassock that partnered the indigo silk sofa as she gave the idea some thought. "No more or less," she said slowly, "than any woman who lives alone." She drew up her knees and curled her legs under her as she leaned on an arm. "Some nutcase could have picked me out at random to frighten."

"But you don't think so."

Andy's wariness increased at his matter-of-fact tone. "No." She watched his gaze stray to the front hall closet where Eric's clothing sprawled suggestively from the opening. She knew what he was think-

ing. He wanted to ask her who they belonged to. He
was out of luck. She never answered unasked questions.

She crossed her arms before her chest, hiking her
cutoff shirt up to expose a sleek two inches of midriff. Victor found his gaze wouldn't move away from
her exposed skin but his mind was still working, after
a fashion. "So, what did the guy want? Did he speak
to you?"

"Loud and clear."

Victor noted the spasm of emotion crossing her
face. She was back to rubbing her arms. Her actions
hiked the tail of her shirt up and down until he felt like
a guy at a peep show. Yet her tone never varied from
sarcasm. "He shoved a knee in my back, smashed my
face to the floor and told me not to move. As if I had
a choice."

Victor didn't allow his mind to linger on what he'd
like to do to the man if he found him. "Anything
else?"

Andy shook her head. "He waited until he thought
I was too terrified to move and then he leapt up and
ran out the door. No, I didn't see his face," she added
quickly. "He was one gigantic male blur."

"What was he wearing?"

"White T-shirt, blue jeans. Sneakers." A gleeful
smile suddenly lit up her bruised features. "He tripped
on the top stair. It's loose. Fell a good part of the way
down. Too bad he didn't break his neck."

Victor smirked but he was curious about what had
made her need to act so hard, seem so tough? *All my
life men have hurt me.* She was unconsciously stroking her swollen jawline. "Tell me about your boyfriend. Where is he?"

The stroking stopped. Her gaze went opaque. "He's dead."

It was time for him to say, "I know," shake her up and get on with the interrogation. But instinct made him hesitate yet again. He told himself he needed more facts before he put her on the defensive. Also, he just wanted to know more about her. "Was he on your list?"

She stood silently gazing into the empty air for so long he began to wonder if and when she'd come back from where her thoughts had taken her. She didn't want to talk about Eric Connors. That much was obvious. Finally, she reached for the silver frame to put it back on the mantel. "Eric was the only man who never hurt me."

Victor was touched, saddened and suddenly jealous of a dead man. A no-win situation. "What happened to him?"

"Auto accident last February."

"That must have been hard for you."

She nodded. "He was a very good friend."

"You loved him?"

Victor saw her reach deep somewhere inside herself for the answer. "Eric was unlike anyone I'd ever met." Her gaze danced toward him and away. "He didn't judge. He thought life was a kick, that people were supposed to have what they wanted." A smile reappeared on her mouth but Victor knew it wasn't for his benefit. "He thought money was the answer to every problem."

"And getting it was his main goal in life?"

She glanced sharply at him. "You would have had to know Eric to understand. He knew how to dream bigger and better than most people."

Victor let his gaze move significantly around the room. Expensive furnishings, Oriental rugs, state-of-the-art sound equipment; Eric and Andrea both believed in living well. "How did he intend to make those dreams real?"

"Are you asking as a federal agent or just asking?"

The attitude in those words whipped Victor's gaze round to meet hers squarely. "Why do you think the Treasury Department would be interested in Eric?"

To Victor's surprise she didn't even hesitate before saying, "I don't." She shrugged again, looking more remote by the second. "It's just that you seem to have only one side, an official one. Can't you hold a conversation without making it sound like an interrogation?"

Victor frowned. He'd heard that question posed a dozen different ways by the people in his life, family, friends, lovers. He had only one answer for them all. "I can try. So, you loved Eric because he could dream big?"

Andy tossed her head. She was in no mood to be grilled but she suspected he would simply leave if she refused to talk and she wasn't ready to be left alone in her violated home, not yet. She could give facts. "Eric not only liked me, he taught me to like myself."

"How?"

She tugged at the bottom of her cutoff shirt, an unusually prim gesture. "I grew up in towns the size of roadside parks. We moved a lot. The only way I survived was by being equal parts dust and spit, and mean as a rattlesnake." She smiled at the look of surprise on his face. "It's true. But when people look at me now they don't see a tomboy from south Texas. They see a sophisticated woman, someone who knows how to dress and talk. I have Eric to thank for that.''

She nodded toward the bookshelves. ''He taught me to recognize true style. Then he showed me how to find quality without paying for it. I learned about wine, exotic cuisines, fashion and art.'' She laughed at some private joke. ''It's amazing how much people take for granted once you give them a few of the right cues.''

Eric had had fine taste in women, Victor allowed him that. Perhaps he had helped her re-create herself. Yet her strangely pathetic story, told in her husky monotone, did not mask what she said about not liking herself before she met Eric. It wasn't much of a leap to suspect Eric had taken advantage of her insecurities. Needy young women were often drawn into a life of crime by men who knew how to make them feel loved. He knew, too, that it took inordinate luck and strength of character to overcome the odds when they were stacked against you. Yet he suspected Andy Uchello could have made it on her own—given the chance.

''So, maybe this Eric taught you a few things,'' he said almost angrily, for he hated the idea that she'd been taken in by a slick Romeo. ''I suppose that made him seem perfect in your eyes, unable to do wrong.''

''No, not perfect.'' As Keisha's recent revelation came to mind, Andy struggled for the right words. ''Eric was far from perfect. He could be a real jerk when something interfered with his plans. And he liked his freedom.'' She ducked his inquiring gaze, feeling she had said too much.

''And he liked money.''

Andy nodded, nudged by old memories.

''Where did the money come from?''

Alarms went off in Andy's head. She had often wondered that herself. But she didn't want to think about it now. After all, Eric was dead. "He worked lots of odd jobs. Couriers don't have regular hours. He had a chauffeur's license, waited tables for caterers of exclusive parties. Things like that. He had a thousand contacts."

"So, you didn't think anything of it when he died."

Andy froze. "What do you mean?"

Victor checked himself. He was moving too fast. "I mean, was it a typical accident, a head-on collision or drunk driving? Something like that?"

"Not exactly." Andy sensed that there was more behind Victor's questions than simple curiosity. "The police called it 'driver's error.' It occurred about 2:00 a.m. on a February morning out at Lake Ray Hubbard. They surmised the wind could have picked up enough lake water to lay a film of ice on the road. His car skidded, lost traction and went into the lake."

She paused, taking a deep breath. She could no longer feel the cooling effects of the air conditioner. It was as if the room had suddenly closed in around her. But she went on because it was impossible not to finish. "No one even knew his car had gone into the lake for three days. A passing trucker noticed something suspicious under the surface of the water."

She shook her head. "They never found the body. Not that it matters. No one could have survived. The police said it sometimes takes . . . months."

Victor was off the sofa in a flash. He only meant to comfort her but the minute he placed an arm around her she turned into him, plowing her head against his shoulder and wrapping her arms about his waist. It was against his better judgment but he enfolded her body against his. She wasn't crying but she trembled with emotion. He supposed he had learned one thing tonight. She had loved Eric Connors. The thought made him envious. She didn't seem the kind to easily offer the trust required for love. He could appreciate that—it was the reason he had never really been in love.

He patted her awkwardly. He knew he should tell her what his office knew about Eric Connors—that he had just been flagged as a suspected freelance courier for Albright when he died. And that his death was listed in their files as a possible homicide. They had their own theory of why Eric's body hadn't been found in the car. They suspected he'd been murdered elsewhere and his car dumped. They couldn't prove it, of course. Yet, if she was working for Albright, that should shake her up enough to get her to tell him all she knew.

But he couldn't do it, not when she was in his arms.

Andy tried to pull herself together. She told herself that the emotion shuddering uncontrollably through her was simply a delayed reaction to all she'd been through that day. She was entitled to a case of nerves but that didn't mean she should wallow in self-pity on the chest of a sexy federal agent.

With a groan of desperation, she pushed away from him, stiff-arming his attempt to draw her back. Because she wanted so very badly to go on hiding in his embrace, the act of will necessary to break away was great.

"I never cry," she said in a low voice as she backed to a safer distance. "I don't know why—I never do that." Her gaze dared him to comment. "It—it's just this damned break-in!" Her jaw clenched in anger. "God! I didn't need this after the day I've had!"

Victor shoved his hands into his pockets, his sooth-ing efforts curtailed. "Problems at work?"

"The pits." Andy tossed her damp fringe of hair to shake off the dregs of emotional distress and began pacing, drawing composure from the simple exercise. "First, my computer crashed. Then, the boss wanted to play footsie over a job possibility." She paused to look up at him with eyes as rich as chocolate syrup. "Then I come home to find everything I possess scat-tered to heck and back."

Victor didn't mean to let it get the better of him but the big yawn caught him by surprise. He thought his jaw would crack before he got it under control.

He looked exhausted, Andy thought, much too tired to be out visiting—unless he had another purpose. The *click* that went off in her mind staggered her. Of course! He was here in an official capacity.

Her eyes narrowed as she asked, "Tough day?"

Victor shrugged, chagrined. "No more or less than usual."

"Then I hope it was worth it."

Victor knew by the tone of her voice that the emo-tional climate between them had taken yet another abrupt shift, this time toward blizzard conditions. Her expression confirmed it. Still, he played dumb. "Worth what?"

She folded her arms and cocked her hip to balance most of her weight on one leg. "You didn't just show up at my apartment, did you? What do you Feds do, listen in on the police bands for kicks?"

Just like that she had stolen his thunder.

Victor hid his chagrin. "We were informed," he said freely. "Do you think it's just coincidence you were robbed so soon after your run-in with the law?"

Andy smirked. "Did you take a good look around as you drove up? Glitz and grit rub shoulders on every corner of Oak Lawn. Robbery is a liability of the neighborhood."

"Do those thieves usually content themselves with threats?"

Andy went very still. "Suppose you explain that."

Victor's expression was grim. For a smart woman she sometimes missed the obvious. "Your place was ransacked but not robbed. That usually means it was meant as a warning. Didn't the police tell you that?"

Andy nodded slowly. They had also asked her if she had any enemies, ongoing disputes with neighbors, things like that. The implication of enemies hadn't rung a bell with her, until now. "You think the break-in might be connected to Albright?"

They were now down to meat and potatoes. Victor took a step toward her. "I'd bet on it. You were very nosy at dinner Saturday night. What's to keep a man suspicious about your interest in his very illegal business from doing a bit of illegal research on you? Maybe he found out something that made him very nervous, something we missed."

"Get out."

"What?"

"Get out. Now." Her anger seemed hard enough to etch glass. "And don't bother coming back. Or, if you decide you must, to bug the place maybe, please leave everything as you found it. The broom and dustpan are in the kitchen pantry."

"You don't think—?" he began testily.

"I'd bet on it," she cut in. "Albright doesn't suspect me of anything except ditziness. But you do, don't you? I think *you* put someone up to this." She swept the room with a hand. "As a warning, as you say. Then you thought you'd waltz in, catch me off guard, and I'd spill whatever dirty little secrets you think I'm keeping. Sorry. You wasted your time.''

Victor didn't even try to untangle the convoluted reasoning she had used to reach that warped conclusion. He couldn't remember a time in the last five years when he'd handled a case more poorly. He felt like a prize ass as well as a frustrated lover. He wanted to cut through the garbage, reach out and bring her back into his arms, show her exactly why he had come here instead of sending Phil. But professionalism gelded his impulse. He had only two choices, accuse her of lying to him, or back off. He had no proof of the first. He headed for the door.

"You're a poor judge of character, Miss Uchello," he tossed over his shoulder. "You tend to back losers."

"Go to hell, Agent Mondragon, and take Albright with you!"

He meant to just leave but a sense of fair play halted him at the door. He turned back. She still stood where he'd left her, looking every inch the tough, aloof woman. "Look. Photos are usually stolen in order to be passed on for identification purposes. Be careful. You still have my card if you decide you'd like to talk."

He saw her chin round in childlike stubbornness. "Don't hold your breath," she said in that husky voice that made the hair on his nape stand on end. "Or, better yet, please do!"

He shook his head. He had tried.

Chapter Eight

Andy begrudgingly counted out the taxi fare in front of her terminal at the Dallas/Fort Worth International Airport. Her courier trip to Seattle was usually an overnighter, so she would leave her car in remote parking and pocket the difference in her transportation allowance. But, upon waking this morning, she had decided to treat herself to a few days of vacation. She was going to stay in Seattle until Sunday morning, away from everything and everyone who could remind her of the first five days of this week. Keisha, bless her, had given her the okay.

She hurried into the terminal building with her roller tote bumping along at her heels. The change in plans had made her run late. She had packed so quickly that she suspected she'd have to purchase a few things once she got there. That didn't matter. She intended to cram every minute of her mini-vacation with activity so that she wouldn't have to think about the night before.

It had taken her half an hour of mixing foundation colors and concealer to hide the ugly bruise on her chin. Now it looked like the result of one heck of a zit instead of a fistfight. People might notice but they wouldn't comment.

She passed security without a hitch and headed for the gate. Messengers for Zane's customers routinely met the couriers inside the terminal so there would be no misunderstanding if the customer's package was detained at security. Once she had escorted a lead-lined case containing ultrasensitive film, which could have been irreparably damaged if opened in light. That sort of complication was better dealt with by the customer's agent. Frequently she carried items the contents of which she had absolutely no knowledge. She was simply the human conduit and watchdog.

"Ms. Uchello?"

Andy nearly collided with the man who stepped into her path, so intent was she on reaching the gate. "I'm so sorry—Mr. Albright!" Recognition startled her more than the near collision but she responded with her usual directness. "What are you doing here?"

"Working." His grin widened as his gaze swept appreciatively over her fitted red sheath dress. "You look great."

"Thanks." Uninterested in exchanging useless compliments, Andy glanced toward the gate posted for her flight. First class and frequent flier passengers were being asked to board. Her nerves tightened a notch as it occurred to her that Victor might have a tail on Albright. This kind of perverted coincidence she did not want to try to explain. She glanced back at Albright. "Are you flying to Seattle?"

He smiled. "No, but I see you are."

"Yes. Business." She craned her head around, looking for the uniform of the bonded messenger service her client most often used. "You must excuse me," she said less than graciously. "My flight's boarding." She started away without even a goodbye.

"Not so fast, Andrea."

She paused, a slight frown registering her dislike of his peremptory tone. When she turned toward him, he was smiling like a blond barracuda, all teeth and predatory gleam.

"I think I have the package you're expecting." He held out a black leather valise.

Clearly stamped across one side was the logo of the company whose package she was to courier. "Where did you get that?" Andy demanded without a care for the way her question was phrased.

He rocked back on his heels, obviously pleased with himself. "I told you at dinner the other night, I'm a courier, too. I just came in on the Chicago flight. I was told to meet a Zane courier but imagine my surprise that it turned out to be you. Small world, isn't it?"

Too damn small for comfort, Andy thought ungenerously. She quickly considered the possibility that what he was telling her was the truth. She had no reason not to believe him, despite what she knew about him. Maybe he had a legitimate courier business on the side. Instinct told her not to pry. But then, she had never been really good at heeding her instincts where danger was concerned. "If what you say is true, why aren't you accompanying the package to Seattle?"

He shrugged. "Ask our boss."

"*Our* boss?"

He waved the valise in his hand. "The customer. I'm just providing the service required."

"I see." Andy reached into her purse and withdrew her company invoice as a flight attendant called for general boarding of the Seattle flight. She didn't have time to quibble. "I assume you have the paperwork?"

"Of course." He produced papers that she carefully compared with her own. This was her package, all right. She glanced up at him. "Amazing."

"Isn't it? Especially since I was going to call you when I got into town. Are you still interested in my offer to throw some extra business your way?"

Andy paused in signing her name to the work sheet. "What?"

He patted his left suit jacket pocket. "I've got another package going to Seattle. If you say yes to delivering it, there's a quick twenty-five hundred in it for you."

Andy cocked a dark brow in skepticism, though she was appalled by his bald approach. What if they were overheard? "What's in it?"

He grinned at her. "You don't really want to know, do you?"

Andy looked away, afraid he would see the panic that had leaped up inside her. *Oh dear God! He was a criminal!*

Until this moment, despite everything—her detainment, threatened arrest, the interest and warnings of Victor Mondragon—she still hadn't really believed it. Now Les Albright was offering her a chance to become a felon, as well. What a deal!

"Your flight's on final call," Albright said as she silently scrawled her name in the appropriate spaces.

"Right." Andy capped her pen and handed him the signed paperwork, and then tucked the courier pouch under her arm. "I've got to go."

"About the other?" His taupe brows rose, underscoring his meaning.

"I don't think—no." Andy shrugged. "Just a coward, I guess. Nice seeing you." She turned and fled so quickly she almost tripped over her tote.

The flight attendant collecting tickets was moving away from the door as Andy hurried up with her pass in hand. "Sorry I'm late."

"You're just in time," the attendant said. She smilingly passed Andy through after verifying her boarding pass.

As she stepped into the jetway Andy's arm was snagged from behind. She whipped around as Albright wedged a manila envelope under her arm next to the courier valise. "You forgot this. Have a good flight, darling," he said loudly as he bent close to kiss her cheek.

Even though Andy flinched away, his lips came within range of her ear to whisper, "If you'd just told me you were a close friend of Eric Connors, you could've saved us the game playing. I'll be in touch." He turned and hurried off at a quick but not noticeably suspicious clip.

"Hey! You can't—" Andy started after him but she was immediately cut off by a passing passenger cart. As she skirted the vehicle, she saw him duck through a nearby exit. She ran after him through the mob of arriving passengers spilling out from the gate adjacent, but it was hopeless. She knew he would be out on the street and gone before she reached the exit. Behind her the flight attendant announced over the loud speaker the final call for the Seattle flight.

"Well, hell!" Andy muttered, startling an elderly couple in her path. "Sorry," she murmured and turned back.

Retracing her steps toward the jetway, she let her anger block out her fear. To blazes with it all! She couldn't miss the flight without good reason or her job would be on the line. Zane Couriers preached the post office's all but abandoned motto as gospel. Rain, sleet, dark of night, personal problems, illness; none of it mattered once a job was accepted. Beside that, she had no earthly idea of how to contact Albright once he'd given her the slip. It would serve him right if she simply tossed the envelope in the trash bin. But she couldn't do that.

Things didn't improve once she boarded the plane. Andy jammed her case into the already stuffed overhead compartment and then noticed with a sinking feeling that she had the misfortune to be seated between two men. Each of them already had his personal computer out and would no doubt be jostling her for elbow room throughout the flight.

"Great!" she muttered, enraged at no one in particular. Then she found a target. Just wait until she got her hands on Jennifer, who booked the company's flights! Jennifer knew about her idiosyncrasy and that she needed a window seat to be comfortable.

With a last desperate hope she glanced up the aisle to find every seat was filled. It was a jumbo jet, carrying nearly four hundred passengers. Where could all these people be going, she fumed in exasperation. With a murderous look, she turned to wedge herself into the middle seat.

She buckled her seat belt, looking neither right nor left to intercept her seat companions' appreciative smiles for the young attractive woman who shared their space. Only when the jet had backed away from the gate did she look at the manila envelope lying in her lap. It looked benign enough. There was no identification on the front. She picked it up and turned it over to make certain. There was no address, no name, no instructions. Nothing. The opening had been sealed with reinforced tape, the kind that could not be tampered with without shredding the envelope. It was a simple but effective device to deter snooping.

If you'd just told me you were a close friend of Eric Connors...

Andy's anger retreated before the echo of Albright's last words. She had pushed them to the back of her mind to keep it operating. Now the memory brought her to a jarring halt. In spite of his casual mention of Eric's name, she had known in her gut that it was nothing less than a threat. But how did Albright know about Eric?

The hair on her arms stood on end as if, as her grandmother liked to say, someone had stepped on her grave.

Victor had warned her that Albright might do some checking up on her.

Andy shut her eyes and tried to remember what her attacker had sounded and looked like. Could it have been Albright? It wouldn't make sense for him to take that kind of risk. A man in his business probably knew lots of people in low places who would do his dirty work for him. He was good at getting people to do what he wanted, as she had already learned to her regret. First, he had persuaded her to pick up his checked bag. Now he had tricked her into carrying a package to Seattle.

Maybe there wasn't an address on Albright's envelope because it didn't need to be delivered. Maybe she would be met at the Seattle airport by some goon

who'd relieve her of it without a word. So much for
the cash payment. She'd be lucky to walk away with
her life. Not that she wanted the money. What she
wanted was to be out of the line of fire.

Andy lunged forward to snag her purse from the
floor. Her hands trembled so badly it took her three
tries to free a credit card from her wallet. She pushed
it edgewise into the slot to release the airphone in the
seat back before her then flipped through her daily
minder for Victor Mondragon's number.

The phone was ringing before she realized she didn't
know what to say to him. Would he believe that she
had accidentally run into Albright and that he had
forced her into carrying—what? She didn't even know
what she had. All she had was the suspicion that it was
stolen merchandise. She knew Victor well enough now
to know how he would respond to her call. He would
more likely suspect that she had agreed to work for
Albright and then panicked. She couldn't produce any
proof to the contrary. She didn't even know how to
contact the man. She pressed the disconnect button
just as someone answered.

She must be really rattled for she hadn't been
thinking straight since the moment Albright appeared. "Oh, God!" she whispered as she fumbled the
phone back into place.

"You okay, lady?" her aisle-side companion inquired.

Andy shot him a hostile look. "Certainly."

The man directed an injured glance her way but she
didn't have the patience to smooth over the moment.
Her brain was in overdrive and she felt as if she had
been swept up in the tail of a deadly Texas twister and,
no matter what she did, she couldn't get away. The

faster it spun the deeper she was being drawn toward disaster. She must think fast if she was to escape!

"Gum? For your ears?" With a leering smile, the man on the aisle offered her a stick of chewing gum.

Andy scorched him with her glance. "No, thank you."

She forgot about the man and made herself concentrate. During the last months of his life Eric had had more money than ever before. He had never explained where it came from, telling her not to worry. Perhaps she should have. Eric wasn't above the occasional shady deal. God knows, he'd helped her by less than legal means. But she never imagined that he might have been involved in genuine criminal activities.

What is forging a birth certificate and background information if not criminal activity? her conscience prompted.

Eric had made it seem a game, like doctoring one's ID in order to drink at a bar before reaching the age of twenty-one. Harmless fun. Nobody was hurt. But Victor Mondragon wouldn't see it that way. If she opened her life one tiny inch to him, he would start digging, if only to verify that she was who she claimed to be. What if he found out that she wasn't?

Andy never noticed the plane leaving the ground. She didn't glance once toward the window, breathless in case the ground wasn't out there somewhere below her view of the horizon. Her life had taken on more weighty issues. If the earth had suddenly and inexplicably dropped away then, at least she was rid of Albright.

"I have to work this out for myself," she murmured under her breath. No Feds, no police of any kind. No one must know what she was into until she could explain convincingly why Albright had approached her. That meant she had to figure out what was going on.

So what if Eric had worked for Albright? What could that mean to her? Had Albright assumed that she, being Eric's live-in girlfriend, knew about his criminal activities? It didn't make much sense that a man in an illegal business would want his employees talking to their significant others about it. Word might eventually leak out to the authorities. Of course, leaks could be patched. What method did Albright use to patch leaks? Threats, or worse? Victor had asked if she hadn't been suspicious of the circumstances of Eric's death. Was it possible—?

Andy shut her eyes. She didn't want to think what she was thinking. She was needlessly scaring herself when she needed to be clearheaded and calm. There was nothing she could do until she reached Seattle. Yet if she didn't stop thinking, she'd be certifiable by the time they touched down. "Oh, Eric," she whispered miserably. "What did you do?"

To stop her thoughts from spinning uselessly, she reached for the in-flight magazine in her seat compartment, trading the manila envelope for it.

"Ms. Uchello?"

Andy jumped at the sound of her name. She'd been engrossed for some time in the puzzle. A flight attendant stood looking at her from the aisle.

"I'm Ms. Uchello," Andy replied.

The young woman smiled. "Would you follow me forward, please?"

"Why?" Andy demanded but she had already reached for her seat belt.

"Just follow me, please." The attendant turned to walk on ahead as Andy squeezed herself out of her seat and into the aisle.

The attendant held the curtain shielding business from coach to allow Andy to pass through then said, "There's a man up in the first-class galley who's requested a private word with you."

Andy turned cold inside. "Who is he?"

The woman shrugged. "Why don't you ask him?"

"What does he look like?"

The flight attendant smiled. "The kind of trouble I'd like to have."

It occurred to Andy as she started down the wide aisle of business class that Albright might have doubled back and gotten on board behind her. Coach passengers on a jumbo jet never even saw first class. Even if that were so, what could he do to her in flight? There were witnesses who could identify him. An attendant knew he'd asked for her. He couldn't push her out a window and he couldn't kill her without incriminating himself. If he just wanted to terrorize her he would find himself fresh out of luck. There was no room left inside her for another single emotion.

But she was wrong.

As she came even with the flight galley Victor Mondragon stepped out of the narrow alley, bristling with menace and masculinity.

"You!"

"Who were you expecting, Ms. Uchello? Your friend, Les?"

Andy felt something lethal if silent go off inside her head. This was the last straw, one surprise too much. She lost it. "I don't know what the hell is going on!" she shouted loud enough for everyone in first class and business to hear. "But I can tell you this much. I feel like a Ping-Pong ball and I'm way past tired of playing the game!" She turned and started down the aisle.

When she felt his hand grasp her arm she swung around, ready to struggle but he propelled her backward and, snatching open the door of a lavatory, shoved her into it. A second later, he followed her in, slamming the door behind himself.

"Okay, Andy," he said against her forehead. "Let's deal."

Andy jerked away from the muffling effect of his broad chest. She might have laughed, if there'd been room for the sound. Airplane lavatories were notoriously small and Victor was a big man. What space there was left was filled by his rage.

"What the hell is it with you?" he demanded on a breath that heated her skin like a west Texas wind in August.

"Me?" Andy shot back, trying and failing to separate herself from his touch. Canned sardines had more personal space. "This is the second time you've pulled me into a bathroom without warning!"

He braced his hands on the bulwark behind her head, his arms forming parallel bars that flanked either side of her. Then he bent down so that they were practically nose-to-nose. He was so close she could see the ebony rings that encircled the molten gold of his irises. "Now, you're going to explain to me exactly what you're doing on this flight when it was booked by Les Albright."

"It wasn't," Andy answered. "The ticket in my purse was issued by Zane Couriers. I regularly fly this route for the office. At least twice a month. Check the books."

"I will." She could feel the anger in him bunching his biceps into mountains on either side of her face. He wouldn't hurt her, she knew. Yet she also knew he was a very angry man at the end of his rope. He wanted to do something quite physical to her. Despite the mess she was in, she had a few opinions about what that should be.

"Look," she began as she tried in vain to scoot back an inch. His thighs were jammed against hers, his belt buckle was leaving an impression on her midriff. "Look," she said again, wondering if they could suffocate in here. "I was just doing my job today when Albright appeared out of the blue."

"He appeared from Chicago," Victor supplied.

"Yes, Chicago," Andy agreed. "That's what he said. You were tailing him?"

"That's not your business."

"Oh really?" she snapped. "After all that's happened I'd not be surprised to learn that you had me followed, as well." The thought made her pause to study his face for a clue. No such luck. "If you did, then you know I'm telling the truth. I wasn't expecting Albright."

"Go on."

"It turns out he had the courier package I was to carry."

"You agreed to carry a package for him?" His pupils expanded so quickly she had the sensation of being drawn into a black hole.

"No, he had the courier package I carried paperwork for. Don't ask me how he got it. All I know is the paperwork I had from Zane Couriers matched the paperwork he presented. I signed and we switched.''

"And then?"

Andy had the disconcerting feeling that she was shrinking then realized her legs were giving way as he pressed in on her. Finally, her bottom met the closed toilet lid.

Victor reached down and jerked her to her feet, bringing nearly every possible inch of their bodies into contact. If that wasn't enough, he lifted a foot and set it on the toilet top, trapping her between his thigh and the sink. "Suppose you tell me why you didn't just walk away and call the cops?"

Andy shifted toward the sink, wishing the rock-hard warmth of his thigh wasn't pressing her hip. Or maybe that wasn't right. But she couldn't afford to think about it. She had to get out of here.

"I tried to call you," she said with a shrug. "Just now. From this plane. Ask my seatmates." She lifted up on tiptoe, hoping to see past him to the door latch but she couldn't get past a rather massive shoulder jammed against the door.

"The time for coyness is over, Andy." He reached out and snagged her lifted chin. That brought her blazing gaze back to his face. "I know you've been lying to me since the moment we met."

"I have not!" she deliberately shouted, hoping her raised voice would draw the attention of the flight attendants. What it did was earn her the broad palm of Victor's hand over her mouth.

"Now, look," he said with menacing calm. "We can do this nicely, or we can do this the hard way. I have a pair of handcuffs and the authority to lock you up in here until we're ready to land. Got it?"

Andy didn't believe him. Not really. But she didn't want to test him at the moment. She nodded. His hand fell away from her mouth. Her voice was subdued. "I took the package and boarded the plane because it's my job." Her gaze again left his face. Avoiding the complete truth was difficult when her opponent's chest was rising and falling against her breasts. "Meeting Albright was an accident unless he planned it."

"Why would he do that?"

Andy looked up at him, stricken by the consequences of the answer. If she lied now, she'd never again have any hope of regaining Victor's trust. Suddenly his trust seemed the only port in the storm her life had become. "I think because he wanted me to carry another package for him."

She felt every muscle in his body tense. Quite impressive. "Something illegal?"

"I don't know. Yes." She fought and won a quick ugly fight with her instinct for self-preservation. "Oh, hell! He offered me twenty-five hundred dollars to take it."

"And you did?"

"No—yes!" So much for honesty! It was like letting snakes out of a basket. The truth seemed to slither away in all directions. "Well, I have it, but it's not what you think," she said angrily.

"What do I think, Andy?"

She looked down, concentrating on the third button on his shirt. "You think I'm a cheap, amoral, money-grubbing gold digger."

"I've never thought you were cheap or grubby," he said softly.

She lifted enormous eyes to his face. "Remind me not to ask you for a character reference."

She thought he nearly smiled. "Cut the bull, Andy. I'm not impressed by your tough talk. I need the truth or the trouble you're in is only going to get worse. What are you carrying?"

"Aside from the fact it's in a manila envelope, I don't know. Albright forced it on me as I was getting on the plane, then disappeared."

"Where is it now?"

"In my seat compartment."

"You left—" For the first time Victor smiled. "Either you're the most naive..." His smile died. "You left it for someone, didn't you?"

It took Andy a moment to catch up with his logic. "You mean you think I left the envelope to be taken by someone else on the flight?" Her expression darkened at his single nod. "You can escort me back to my seat and I'll hand the damned thing to you."

"Not necessary."

Whatever impulse toward generosity she thought she had seen in his gaze moments before was gone. As she looked into Victor Mondragon's eyes she remembered that gold was just a metal and even precious metals were cold.

Frustration made Andy react. She struck him with a fist in the solar plexus. She sometimes sparred in the boxing ring for exercise but her punch was shortened by the lack of room. Still, surprise made it very effective. He made a *whoof* sound and staggered a full half inch backward.

"You really think I'm a creep, don't you?" she snapped at him, not caring that she might be overheard. "Just because I don't fit your Boy Scout profile of a model citizen doesn't mean I'm a louse and a liar." She stuck her chin out, barely wincing at the pain the bruise there caused her. "I'm the victim here! You're the law. You're supposed to be protecting *me*, damn it!"

She didn't see the door open but one moment she was being dragged in against the wall of his chest, the next she was being propelled backward into the hallway by the first-class galley. He slammed the door shut in her face.

Andy reached for the door latch as the occupied sign slid into place along with the lock. "Damn!" She struck the door with the toe of her shoe then turned and stalked back down the aisle, offering no explanation but an angry expression to the curious passengers watching her.

How dare he think the worst of her just because she hadn't behaved as he thought she should? He didn't know how much she wanted to live up to his expectations and how impossible it was.

By the time she reached her row her aisle-side companion had popped up like a jack-in-the-box. The man by the window kept his head bent over his laptop, which was just as well. She already felt as if she'd been thoroughly molested, though Victor Mondragon hadn't even kissed her!

Meanwhile in first class, Victor returned to his first-class seat and let his anger abate. Andy Uchello was the most infuriating female he had ever met. Suspects never got to him. Yet, she made him want to do things like punch walls and throw furniture. He hadn't known from one second to the next whether he would let her go unharmed or release his rage in the absolutely inappropriate form of a ravishing embrace. The rules of his job required that he be circumspect. Yet

Andy Uchello goaded him time and time again to indiscretion.

"You're losing it, Vic!" He wiped a heavy hand down his face. He had to give her credit. No one pulled off innocent outrage better than she did. It was a great performance. He wished he could believe it. But facts were facts and the latest of them indicated that now more than ever she couldn't be trusted.

After he'd left her ransacked apartment, he'd gone back to the office. Phil was waiting for him with the deep background check he had ordered before going to see Andy. It had made for very enlightening if not disheartening reading. It seemed Andrea Uchello had a paper trail that went back exactly three years, the amount of time she had been in Dallas. Before that, the name disappeared from all easily accessible government files. It seemed that she had arrived fully grown into the world.

The facts saddened him, even while he told himself he should have expected something like it. He'd run into this kind of thing before, with criminals who wished to relieve themselves of their damaging records or people who had for whatever reason decided to drop out of their former lives.

There were lots of reasons people changed their identities. Unfortunately, the most common ones involved trouble with the law. Andy certainly was in trouble now. Before leaving Dallas, he had given Phil the assignment to discover just who she really was.

Victor reclined in his seat, enjoying the comfort of real leather. It almost canceled out the hassle of the last days. He'd had almost no sleep after a call had come in from the Chicago office during the night, informing him that Albright had booked a dawn flight for Dallas. Still hopeful of infiltrating Albright's ring, he had decided to chance intercepting him in Dallas and following him to Seattle.

He had been observing the boarding passengers from the first-class galley when he spotted Andrea Uchello. Albright wasn't aboard but she was. The story she'd told him had more holes in it than a piece of Swiss cheese. He believed only one element of it. She was genuinely frightened.

Now more than ever he needed the answer to who she really was. He hoped the answer to that question and a few others would be waiting for him when the flight touched down in Seattle.

Chapter Nine

Andy stepped into the inviting lobby of the Seattle Sheraton, which was deliciously bright and airy on this rare sunny afternoon. Her regular delivery to Sunn Company Inc. had gone smoothly, as always. Following company policy, she had gone there straight from the airport. Now she had the rest of the day to herself. Usually, she had a routine when in Seattle. After checking in at her hotel, she most often went for a walk down to the docks. But today, she didn't even think about walking.

Perhaps it was just her own strained nerves but she was pretty certain she was being watched. She'd become so suspicious by the time she left Sunn Company's offices that she had waved on the first three taxis who stopped for her. Even after deciding that she was being a fool, she had nearly asked the driver whose cab she entered if he worked for Victor's department. Of course, he would have thought she was nuts. Maybe she was. That would explain why she was walking around Seattle with an envelope filled with God-only-knew what sort of felonious matter inside.

She glanced around the hotel lobby, daring anyone to make eye contact. The area was nearly empty. At

12:45 p.m. it was a bit late for checkout and too early for the check-in rush. There were two groups of well-dressed ladies standing nearby chattering about where they should have lunch. A few men in business suits stood impatiently glancing at either the main doors or the elevators. Victor Mondragon was nowhere in sight. Not that she was expecting him to be. When he'd allowed her to leave the plane and then the terminal without approaching her or having her detained, she decided he had crawled back into the woodwork, so to speak, to wait and see what she would do next.

"Take a long hot bath and change clothes," Andy murmured.

"I beg your pardon?" responded the desk clerk whom she'd approached.

Andy placed her company voucher on the counter. "I have a reservation. I'd like a room with a king-size bed, no smoking, preferably with a whirlpool and bar."

The young woman smiled. "Tough day, already, Ms. Uchello?"

"And going to get rougher," Andy replied, guardedly pleased that she'd been recognized. Sunn Company kept a standing room reservation available for their out-of-town customers' use. Andy had stayed here at least a dozen times in the past eight months. Once she had dreamed of being recognized by the staff of fine hotels all over the world. Now she craved anonymity.

The clerk was remarkably efficient. Within a matter of minutes Andy was handed a room key and a key to the bar.

"You also have a message," the desk clerk said as she handed Andy a sealed white business-size envelope.

"Who left it for me?" Andy demanded. Tact had deserted her hours ago.

"I don't know. I wasn't on duty when it came in. Would you like me to ask?"

Andy shook her head. What difference did it make? Whether Albright or Mondragon, it wasn't going to be good news.

The clerk smiled. "Here comes a bellman to escort you."

"Thank you." Andy turned to follow the young man who took over the wheeling of her case. She glanced at the white envelope. Her name was written neatly on the back. "Just a minute." As the bellboy paused she turned back to the desk. "I'd like to put something in your vault."

A few minutes later she rejoined the bellboy, feeling lighter in heart and mind. The manila envelope from Albright was where no one could get it without her cooperation. That should provide some kind of security.

THE SOUND OF RAIN pelting the windows awakened her. She lay facedown and catercorner across the enormous hotel bed. From this vantage point she could just make out the numbers on the digital clock on the nightstand—4:32.

With the curtains drawn, the room was in near darkness. She had slept deeply, the kind of slumber that left her feeling not quite certain of her surroundings. The thick terry-cloth bathrobe that had been provided for her use was as good as cuddling a teddy bear, Andy decided as she flipped over on her back. After a long soak in the tub with the whirlpool blasting away every kink and worry, she had finished off an icy cold beer from the bar and then fallen asleep.

She realized she had not slept this soundly in days. For three short blissful hours Albright, Mondragon and illegal courier rings did not exist. She had gone home in her dreams, home to her grandmother's modest house in Yard, Texas, where once, long ago, she had been happy.

Mamma, as she called her grandmother, had owned orange and grapefruit orchards, grew watermelons and sorghum for commercial sale. It had been a small farm, the chance to turn a profit depending on weather, luck and timing. After she was abandoned as a baby by her mother, the farm had been the only home Andy had known, her grandmother her only family. Then, when she was ten, a man had come to Yard with a court order declaring that he was her father.

Andy bit her lip and drew her knees in against her chest to protect herself against the remembered pain. Her father had come for her, demanding the right to raise his own child. She never saw her grandmother again. After that, her life became mere existence. Her father was a labor contractor for seasonal workers who sold his services all over southwest Texas. She lived in a dozen different places the next five years and hated every one. She was considered a migrant worker's child, rootless with an untraditional life-style in a part of the U.S. that still believed in the sanctity of home, mom and apple pie. Then she had done the unforgivable by turning on her own kin.

Andy slung an arm over her eyes, willing the co-cooning darkness to keep all thoughts at bay. But the world wouldn't stay away forever. Now, as before, there was something drawing her back to reality. Right now that something was the clean white business envelope propped up on the pillow by her head. She couldn't avoid its reality forever, even if that was exactly what she wanted to do.

She reached for it reluctantly, held it above her head as she tore off a narrow end, and then blew into it to balloon it open. As she held it up a single slip of paper drifted down onto the bed.

Andy turned back onto her stomach and propped her chin on her fists, not wanting to touch the paper. A Vancouver address had been typed on it, along with a single line that read, "This location will receive the package." The paper didn't indicate from whom it was, nor did it give a time for the delivery. There wasn't even a contact. She had to admire Albright's ingenuity. Even if she ran screaming to the police, what could she give them but the package and an address? She couldn't even say with certainty who'd left the message, the client or Albright. Nothing but her word—shaky under the circumstances—connected Albright to the actual transaction.

She thought of Victor and how angry he had been to find her aboard the Seattle flight. She had been shaken by the realization that he was on board, not for any reason connected to her trouble with the law. She hadn't forgotten one second of what it felt like to be in his arms. Though his gifted kisses could not be overlooked, what remained indelibly on her mind was the feeling of safety, the absolute rightness of his touch. It hadn't been simply a matter of her libido responding to his impressively masculine body and mutual attraction. In his arms she had experienced the sense of coming home to a place she had never been. That somewhere was a safe haven.

"Don't think about it!" she commanded herself.

Her response didn't make any sense. Even so, the one person on the entire planet she wished would knock on her door right now was Victor Mondragon. She might fear the trouble he would cause her in the name of justice, but she also knew that if she could just earn his trust, he could be counted on. She needed help, someone to confide in, someone to believe her. She needed Victor.

But that was a pipe dream.

His department suspected Albright but Victor had told her that until they had hard evidence that would hold up in court, they couldn't pick him up. As things stood, the only solid tie to the package Albright had thrust on her was herself. If the contents of the manila envelope was felonious, that made her an accessory to a crime. She cringed inside. She knew all too well what that would mean. She'd be taken into custody, if only until the authorities could check out her story. Meanwhile they'd dig up her past and then Victor would know what a liar she was. Any hope of convincing him she was innocent would be lost.

Andy hid her face in her hands. "I can't do that!" So, she would do nothing.

She didn't want any part of this mess, hadn't asked to be drawn into the tangle of deception. For one hot minute the morning after meeting Albright, she had thought she would turn crusader, help Mondragon get the bad man. But that, too, was only wishful thinking. She was no do-gooder. She would only have brought the law down on her own head. Now, she only wanted to get away from the whole situation before it destroyed her. But at every turn, something kept dragging her back in, deeper and more dangerously.

So, maybe it was time *she* did a disappearing act.

She reached for the phone and punched the operator's button. "Connect me with your travel service, please."

Five minutes later she was cinching in the belt on her metallic gold raincoat. Every flight to Dallas on every carrier was booked solid for the rest of the day. She could try standby, but that meant an endless wait and she'd had enough of rude surprises at airport terminals to last her the rest of her life. Her only alternative was to wait for a morning flight. Waiting alone in her room made her feel like a sitting duck. If she didn't get out of here, she would suffocate.

Despite the rain, which had quickly turned from a late summer squall into a light mist that made downtown Seattle seem like an Impressionist painting come to life, Andy enjoyed her walk down to the waterfront. The wonderful Pike Place Market was not only a prime tourist attraction but a genuine fish and produce market where the day's catch, farm-to-market fruits and vegetables, as well as huge bouquets of flowers could be had for a reasonable price. At this time of day it was alive with late shoppers who'd dropped by after work to pick up a piece of fresh salmon or King crab for their dinner.

To cheer herself up Andy bought an armful of snapdragons the colors of which ranged from bright lemon, pink and white to deep mauve, magenta and bronze. The vendor wrapped them in a print paper cone to keep them moist. She then treated herself to an early dinner of steamed crabs in one of the many restaurants that shared space with the market. She browsed a long time through stalls selling handmade crafts and locally produced jellies and jams, letting her mind drift far from the worries that had preoccupied her for days.

Afterward, she headed out to walk along the harbor front for several blocks. She knew from past visits that on warm sunny days the area was filled with vendors and local artists spilling out across the lawn of the adjacent park. But the weather had chased them off. She paused to watch as the ferry from Seattle to Bainbridge Island disappeared into the mist of Puget Sound, its multiple decks sprouting the colorful mushrooms of commuters' umbrellas. To the south, the snow-crested peak of Mount Rainier floated almost mystically above the mountain ridge as the late-afternoon sun peeked out from beneath the passing rain clouds to spotlight it.

As she strolled aimlessly on, her face kissed by salt mist, the smells and beauty of the northwest Pacific crowded in to remind her that Zane had made her an offer that would allow her to move here. At the time she had been distracted by petty concerns like his pointed interest in her and the implied obligations of her acceptance. Now those things seemed minor irritations that she could easily deal with. Eric's death had put her future on hold. She needed to start over. Seattle seemed a great place in which to do it.

By the time she had turned back toward town and finished the steep climb up from the harbor to the hotel, she was ready to call Zane. But the two-hour time change meant that he had long ago left his office. As the twilight closed in about her, she hugged her luscious bouquet to her chest and smiled. In spite of everything she had been through this week, life didn't seem so bad when she was surrounded by such beauty.

She reached a crowded intersection just as the Don't Walk light began to flash. She lifted her head, trying to judge if she'd have enough time to dash across when, with the unexpectedness of a lightning bolt, she saw him.

Eric Connors!

He stood on the opposite street corner, ready to cross the avenue perpendicular to where she waited. "Eric!" She didn't stop to think but started after him.

Hands dragged her back toward the safety of the curb just as a car shot past with a warning blare of its horn. Andy felt the heat of the engine's exhaust on her legs.

"Didn't you see the light change, miss?" demanded the businessman in a mackintosh who had pulled her out of harm's way.

"I—I..." Andy swallowed as her body reacted with a hard shudder to the near collision. Her gaze hung doggedly onto the image of the man moving away from her, but he was already being swallowed up by the steady stream of rush-hour traffic and pedestrians.

"You must be more careful in future, dear," said the elderly woman on her right.

Embarrassed, Andy stumbled to the back of the crowd and took a sudden left, hurrying to cross with the light.

She put her head down and began to jog, her shoes making *splish-splash* sounds as she trampled through the many puddles on the sidewalk. Anger and shame warred within her. Anger, as always, won out.

How stupid she had been to make that pitiful mistake again! How many times during the weeks following Eric's death had she thought she'd seen him in Dallas, on the street or in a club in Deep Ellum? More than once she'd hurried right up to the man before realizing that it wasn't, couldn't be, Eric. It was only a trick of the light. A recurring mirage. Eric was dead. She knew that!

She crushed her bouquet in her arms, uncaring that the bruising made blossoms drop from it. The pleasure of her late-afternoon stroll was spoiled. Her nerves had reformed into knots twice as tight and half as steady as before. Yet she went on castigating herself as she slowed to a walk because it was better to be angry than scared. Earlier she had thought she was being followed and just now she thought she saw a dead man. Her senses and her instincts weren't to be trusted.

She was completely lost before she realized she had wandered away from the hotel. The steep narrow streets had emptied quickly of traffic. She turned up the quietest of them.

The violet shadows formed by the canyon walls of buildings made the air suddenly much cooler here. In the distance behind her she heard foghorns out on the water.

It began to rain in earnest again but she didn't bother to use her umbrella this time. The steady hiss both muffled and enhanced sounds, seemingly at random. Full traction eluded the soles of her sneakers on the slickest part of the climb. San Francisco's steep streets had nothing on Seattle, she thought as she tried to dig in her heels.

The footsteps coming up behind her didn't alarm her because at that moment a couple turned into the street from the opposite end and began walking toward her. No one would dare accost her in full view of witnesses.

Then a hand on her arm caused her to jump. Gathering breath to scream, she spun around, ready to use her rolled umbrella as a weapon.

"You!"

The sight of Victor Mondragon was a complete and devastating shock. It stripped her of any sense of self-preservation or caution. He was dressed in a dark blue nylon jogging suit. Rain sluiced from the ends of his loose black hair onto his shoulders. He was as wet as she was, yet he didn't seem to care. She reached out and touched his grim rain-drenched face, summoning the last smile she had left in her to welcome him.

He didn't even hesitate but pulled her quickly in against him. Like partners on the dance floor, he waltzed her backward into the alcove of a closed storefront, pressing them both into the shadowy depths of the darkened doorway. Then he looked down at her and smiled.

They didn't speak, they didn't need words. Andy knew he understood that words would only get them in trouble. They needed what words wouldn't give them, a chance.

His fingers raked carefully through her short hair, slicked down by rain, to push the sopping strands back from her face. Then his fingers skimmed her brow and cheeks to remove the dampness. She felt his body crush the bouquet she still held between them as he bent to her. His wet cheek slipped sleekly across hers. And then his lips, cool and firm, settled over hers.

His kiss was tender, unlike the rapacious hunger of the first they had shared. But the undercurrent of need remained and she answered it with a hunger of her own. Openmouthed and unselfishly, she surrendered to his lead, enjoying the unique taste and texture and heat of him.

Like bells on the breeze she heard the approving laughter of the passing couple and knew how it must seem, that she and Victor were two eager lovers finding in the opportunity of shelter the chance to further their romance.

After a moment she stepped back from him and released the soggy flattened paper funnel of snapdragons. The flowers scattered about their feet as she reached up to unzip his jacket. Smiling, he undid the knot in her raincoat. Then he pulled her in again, his hands on her waist beneath her coat. As their lips met, she surged gently into him, her breasts pillowing on his shirtfront as her hips cradled his. Her hands went inside his jacket to circle his waist and then slide up the expanding contours of his back to hug him even closer.

The kisses spun out. There was no urgency like before when each was racing against the pangs of conscience. His body was warm against hers, feeding his heat and energy directly into her rain-chilled skin. It was as if he knew just what she needed and it was exactly what he wanted to give her.

Dear Lord! Was this really happening? Her eyes opened. His were sealed shut. A thick fringe of black satin lashes lay tenderly against his upper cheeks. The sight was inexpressibly precious to her.

His hands moved down over the full curves of her derriere where they cupped and lifted her toward him. There was no pretense in what he wanted. She mimicked his action. Her fingers slid down over the tight compact globes of his buttocks and then flexed, making indentations in his firm flesh. He groaned in response, straining against her as if he would make love to her through their clothing.

He pressed her to the wall, blocking out the world and all in it but the soft, love sounds of their kisses and the faint hissing rain.

Finally he lifted his head, his fingers moving up to frame her face as he said, "Let's get out of here!"

Andy stared back into the dark pools of his eyes. "Where?"

His smile was so warmly intimate it glowed in the dimness. "You'll see!"

He took her by the hand and pulled her along with him back down toward the harbor.

It didn't matter that they were half drowned by the time they reached the harbor where dozens of boats were anchored. He led her down one of the many piers almost to the end. Finally he paused and then jumped down onto the bow of a small sailboat. He turned to lift her down and then opened the hatchway and motioned her down steps into the dim, unlit cabin. He followed, closing the hatchway behind him.

Andy barely noticed her surroundings before he came up and embraced her from behind, one hand finding the fullness of a breast, the other going lower to press her hips into his groin with the intimate pressure of his hand in front. His lips found her neck, gently sucking her damp skin.

Andy tilted her head back, her arms moving backward to grasp and hold him close. He managed to pull her raincoat off without losing contact with her and then he turned her to face him. He slowly opened the buttons of her blouse, kissing each new inch of skin that was revealed. When he encountered the lace edge of her bra she heard him murmur in pleasure and the hot tip of his tongue licked under the lace, leaving a sleek, wet trail across the upper curve of one breast. Then he gently peeled back her blouse to expose the other side and kissed her low down between the mounds, his tongue stroking the cleft.

"You smell so good," he said, his voice muffled by her skin, and kissed her again. "I want your scent on my skin."

He removed her blouse and then her bra, pausing to salute each ripe breast with a tonguing kiss. As he knelt before her, his fingers fanned out across her abdomen, the tips brushing the underside of each breast. Then his fingers worked the button of her waistband and lowered the zipper of her jeans, exposing the lace wedge of her panties. The material of her clothing followed the downward pressure of his hands to her ankles. Finally he leaned in close, grinding his face in the soft warmth of her lower belly as his hands encircled her hips.

"You're sweet and soft," he whispered, as if he spoke only to himself. Indeed, he began to speak softly in Spanish for it seemed English could no longer adequately accommodate his feelings.

Andy bent and cradled his head in her hands, feeling a sense of joy and sweet stabbing desire new to her experience. When he rose again to his feet, he picked her up and carried her a short distance.

As he bent with her, Andy put out a hand and encountered a sheet with the firmness of a mattress beneath. She could not clearly see the bed but it didn't matter. He had stepped back and she watched his silhouette quickly divest itself of clothing. And then he was touching her again. He pushed her flat on the mattress, following the pressure of his hands with the solid hard length of his body.

Even then he did not rush them. He licked and tasted and kissed and tongued her until it seemed her skin was afire and low down the gnawing hunger was unbearable. Eagerly she gave as good as she got, stroke for stroke, kiss for kiss, lick for lick. The warm dark secret places of his body smelled wonderfully clean and musky and masculine.

He seemed to know the moment she could stand no more. She felt him pause and knew what he was doing. Even now he was thinking for both of them, protecting her even though she had forgotten to think or ask.

She reached for him, touched him and said, "Thank you."

He answered her with a kiss as he found her and entered her welcoming liquid-lined warmth.

He worked against her beautifully, whispering words of encouragement and approval. Always before Andy had become stiff and uncertain of herself at this point, not knowing what was expected of her beyond compliance. But Victor would not let her retreat into herself. He tugged at her nipples until she gasped in need and then stroked her inside and out until she was vocalizing the pleasure he gave her. There was no time to doubt herself, to retreat from the brink or hesitate and lose the joy. He praised her, murmured his pleasure in her fulfillment, then joined her in the blissful release.

Then he did the most remarkable thing of all. Instead of rolling off and away from her, he pulled her with him until they lay on their sides face-to-face and held her tightly as their hearts slowed and their breathing returned to normal.

Andy choked in her laughter, tears starting in her eyes. She had never before shared in loving so unselfishly and generously. *Dear Lord,* she silently prayed, *don't let me lose him!*

It had to come, the moment when reality had to be faced. It happened in the simple action of Victor switching on the light.

As the features of the tiny cabin jumped into focus, Andy rolled away from him onto her back. "Where are we?"

"Aboard official government property."

"A yacht?"

"Nothing that fancy. It's a sailboat, used mostly for stakeouts. It gives us certain maneuverability, this being a harbor community. Right now, it's my home away from home."

"I suppose my being here could get you in trouble."

He smiled with the amazed delight of a boy who'd accomplished a supposedly impossible feat. "Hell! I'm so far over the line this time I'm not sure I know where it is anymore."

Andy lay perfectly still. "And that bothers you."

"No. Yes." He touched her face with the gentlest of touches. "I can't afford to be wrong about you."

She wondered if he was thinking of his reputation or his job, or both. Or was he thinking of himself? Please, let it be the last.

She laid her hand palm-flat on his smooth, deep bronze chest. The steady rhythm of his heart comforted her fear. "If your department learns about us, will they take your badge?"

His smile didn't falter. "I imagine there'd be some sort of disciplinary action. Probably a desk job in D.C. for a while, something designed to drive me up the wall with boredom."

"Is that all?"

He shrugged, the up and down action of his heavy shoulder muscles stealing her attention. "I won't lie and say I don't care about my job or what happens next. I have work to finish and until I think I can no longer function effectively—or my partner turns me in for 'conduct unbecoming'—I'm staying on the case."

Andy looked into his golden eyes and saw herself reflected in them. "Even if it could destroy us?"

His eyes darkened. "Will it?"

Andy looked away. "I honestly don't know. Maybe. Probably. But not because of any connection with Albright." She glanced back at him, willing him to believe her. "There are . . . other reasons."

His scowl deepened. "Like Eric Connors?"

She smiled. He was jealous! Good. It meant his emotions were involved. So, heaven help her, were hers. "Eric's part of the past. I've needed to get over—well, that part of my life." She leaned in to nuzzle his neck with her nose. "I think what we've shared proves I am."

He bent over her, bringing the sexy slant of his mouth into more illegal contact with hers. By the time he lifted it her heart was racing and her breath was choppy. Looking down, he touched one of her hardened nipples and smiled. "I think maybe you're right."

Andy swatted his hand away. "You think quite a lot of your abilities, don't you?"

He didn't come back with the smug comment she expected. His face remained serious. "There's no one else in my life. Hasn't been for a while. It's a liability of my job. Most women don't like waiting while that job comes first."

Andy smiled as she waltzed her fingers down his stomach. "Then they're missing a serious good time."

He caught her hand just above the silky hairs of his groin. "Is that what this is, a good time?"

It was Andy's turn to frown. "I don't know what it is."

"What do you want it to be?"

"Don't!" She touched a finger to his lips. "Just let it be, okay? Just let *us* be."

"All right." He nipped the tip of the finger she had laid against his mouth. "For now."

As he released her hand, she saw for the first time the tattoo on the inner side of his left forearm. "What's this?"

Victor glanced down at the crudely designed dagger. "It's a reminder of my misspent youth."

"You?" Andy countered in amusement. "Mister Dudley Do-right, always-gets-his-man? You have a past?"

Victor held her mocking gaze. "I grew up in L.A. The dagger was the emblem of my gang. Every drop of blood represents an enemy defeated."

Andy's gaze dropped to his forearm. There was a single dot below the knife point. Her gaze rose only as far as his rib cage where a corrugated scar skimmed the edge of his lowest rib. She ran a finger over its silvery length. "And this?"

"A rival gang member jumped me with a knife." His face had gone smooth, devoid of any emotion. "I didn't mean to kill him but he sure wanted to kill me."

"It was self-defense," Andy answered automatically for him.

His eyes bored into hers. "Maybe. That's what my folks said. Even the police agreed. But after I stopped shaking and crying myself to sleep every night, I discovered that I wasn't over the thrill of being a gang member. That kid's death had given me stature in the community."

He shook his head, as if he were talking about some poor loser, not himself. "It's a funny thing about fame. It's easy to get hooked on the feeling of power, the respect, the attention even a bad reputation can earn you."

Andy held her breath. Those words could have been hers. Hadn't she thought the very same thing, just before she'd learned the downside of a bad rep?

"Girls wanted to be seen with me, wanted to say they'd slept with me. But it wears off quickly. Another murder happens. There's another hero in the barrio. You're history unless you can keep upping the ante."

"And did you?"

He smiled. "I suppose you could say I got lucky. I got arrested for robbery."

He sounded serious but she couldn't help wondering if this was some new tactic. "You've done jail time?"

"You look surprised. What's the matter, are you about to object to having an ex-con as a lover?"

Eyes bright with fear, Andy said, "Wouldn't you?"

He stared at her, his golden eyes glowing like torches. "So, a barrio guy isn't good enough for you. That never occurred to me." As he sat up his body language became tense. "As I said, a dangerous reputation can be a turn-on for some women. For others it's a crime that no amount of restitution can erase." His tone was glib, as if his words didn't matter. "I just didn't figure you for the second type."

The unfair accusation stung Andy to the core. She struck back the only way she knew how, with the same self-defeating aggression that had wrecked her life more than once.

She sat up, ignoring her nudity and his. "What type did you think I was?" Sarcasm made her words sharp and ugly. "Let me guess. The kind that sees as fair game any sleazeball with a fat wallet."

The anger that leaped into his expression paralyzed her. He lunged at her and pushed her back onto the bedding, pinning her there with his palms. "Don't do this! It's unworthy of you, of what we've shared." His golden eyes blazed with outrage but she sensed it was directed at her temper, not at her. "I'll accept your prejudice against my past." His pressure on her shoulders eased. "I should have told you sooner but—*Dios!*—when have we had a moment to act like ordinary people?"

"Never," she answered in an emotion-racked voice. "Because we're not an ordinary couple. We're breaking every rule either of us ever made for ourselves." Her hand snaked up and strongly cupped the back of his neck. "But I don't care, if you don't."

She watched him mentally sift through all the sane reasons why he should just put on his pants and leave—or better yet, put her out. At close range it wasn't pleasant viewing. The conclusion did not ease the heavy lines bisecting his brows. "Is there something you want to tell me, Andy?"

No. Yes. A thousand things. Explanations. Excuses. Pleadings for understanding. Andy shook her head. "It's not at all what you think, my feelings about your past." She stroked his hair at the back of his neck. "You, at least, outlived your mistakes. Most people can't."

"I didn't do it alone." His expression relaxed. "My parents were poor but they were also community leaders. They had political influence. Thanks to the intervention of a state representative they approached, I found myself in a military-style boarding school in Louisiana instead of prison."

He grinned. "I couldn't tell the difference at first. I hated the first year. All that kept me from running away was the memory of my mother's face when she and my father put me on the bus for that school. She'd looked haunted, as if she were sending me away forever. I couldn't imagine what it would have done to her if I had been on my way to doing hard time. I had to make her sacrifice count for something. After getting the attitude kicked out of me I discovered I had a brain. From high school I went into the military for three years. Then college made sense. I joined the agency right after graduation."

Andy envied him the chance to start over. "You're lucky to have had family who cared so much about you."

His expression sharpened. "Didn't you?"

She looked away. "I told you, benign neglect."

He palmed her cheek, turned her face back to his. "Want to tell me about it?"

Andy shook her head. "I don't talk about it. Ever."

"Then answer a different question."

Andy braced herself. "If I can."

"Albright's in Seattle. Will you help me set a trap for him?"

Chapter Ten

Andy sat in her hotel room the next morning and waited.

Albright had called, just as Victor predicted he would if she didn't deliver the envelope. Albright had sounded testy, saying he had received a call from the disgruntled client whose package had failed to show. He said he was calling from a plane en route to Seattle, yet she knew, thanks to Victor's surveillance team, that Albright was already in Seattle, staying at a motel at the edge of the city. Was the fiction of his coming in on a morning flight meant to throw her off his trail? Or was it a precaution to keep her from suspecting that he had been following her? Victor said it didn't matter, as long as Albright showed up.

Andy held on to her last image of Victor for courage. He'd been standing in the galley of the sailboat, a pair of unzipped jeans riding the jut of his hipbones. Otherwise he'd been naked, his lips still damp from their last lingering kiss. He had said they couldn't leave together. If Albright was suspicious, he might be watching the hotel. He would have her followed himself, at a safe distance.

"I hope you know what you're doing, Victor," she whispered.

It was now strictly a war of nerves. It had been easy for her to tell Albright the story Victor had suggested. It was nothing less than the truth: she didn't want anything to do with "special packages" or earning extra money. The tremor in her voice didn't have to be faked, either. She was afraid of Albright and of what would happen next.

She reached into her purse for her lipstick. She twisted it open and began to apply it blindly to her already perfectly colored mouth. She had told Albright that she'd had enough, that he would have to come and get the envelope if he wanted it. She would leave a message at the desk, giving him the right to retrieve it from the hotel vault. She had done almost everything Victor had asked of her. Except for one thing.

Andy closed her lipstick and placed it back in her purse. She'd spent an extraordinary night with Victor, a once-in-a-lifetime revelation about the nature of love. She had fallen hard, so hard and deep that for the first time in years she was thinking about someone other than herself. Victor didn't require her cooperation to catch Albright but she wanted to help him even if, ultimately, it cost her everything: her reputation, her job, and—most of all—Victor.

Less than a week ago her world had been turned upside down by a chance encounter. Suddenly, everything she thought she had escaped from had come back to haunt her. She had spent years running from things, from people's opinions, from feelings of guilt and self-loathing, from her own fears. She had even tried to outrun her own past.

The last thing Victor had told her to do was leave the hotel before Albright arrived. She couldn't do that. It was time she faced things, faced herself. It was time she stopped running.

She had told Victor she wanted to face Albright. She hadn't explained but she wasn't doing it for the reasons of right and wrong Victor had encouraged her with. She needed to prove to herself that she could face the consequences of her actions, face an enemy and walk away with her head held high. She wanted to prove herself worthy of Victor's trust, and his faith in her.

But it wasn't working.

She felt sick and numb with fear, and very ashamed. Now that Victor was no longer beside her, his presence cushioning her thoughts as well as her body, that stark awareness of what she was about to do had brought back memories.

Once before she had set a man up for a federal bust. That man was her father.

No matter how she twisted it around in her mind— and she had become a pro at making pretzel shapes of her conscience—the comparison couldn't be avoided. Spinning the old tapes, as Keisha liked to say about reliving mistakes and regrets. She couldn't stop them. God knows, she had tried.

Andy clasped her arms to her body, as if a sudden chill had entered her hotel room, and began to pace. The old tapes were running as images flickered like quick cuts from an MTV video at the back of her vision.

After five years of knocking around south Texas farms and cattle ranches with her father, Jake Trask, she'd seen the worst side of every dusty town in the

Rio Grande Valley between Raymondville, Texas, and Reynosa, Mexico. Each harvest season, her father got a semipermanent job as a labor broker of migrant workers who came to pick produce. This was the time she hated the most. He was often gone for days with no prior warning or explanation when he returned. But she was no fool.

Years earlier she'd learned that her father was paid to smuggle illegal aliens across the Mexican border to harvest crops. It was dirty, dangerous work. The Border Patrol was always on the lookout for smugglers. Everyone knew and talked openly about how it was impossible to adequately patrol the vast, empty ranch and farmland with anything less than several legions of armed men. So her father's business had thrived, but she hated it. An itinerant herself, she was always the new face in the classroom, enduring unmerciful teasing about her shabby clothing and her vagabond life-style. During those years all she had wanted her father to do was settle down. But he ignored her. So she started praying that something would happen.

The summer she turned fifteen, something did. She fell in love. He was a young drifter several years her senior, hired by the same farmer who'd hired her father. His name was Jess. He hit it off with her father but he seemed more interested in hanging around her house when her father was absent, and that was fine. He had nice manners and he looked at her the way a man looks at a pretty girl. She had cooked for him, mended a torn shirt, started packing his lunches. She knew her crush amused him, but he never made fun of her. For that alone, she worshiped him.

She'd have done anything to impress him. So, one night when Jess came by during one of her father's absences, she told him that her father often did "special" jobs. With his encouragement, she'd finally confided the nature of her father's criminal activities and how much she hated them.

Andy paused in her pacing. She could remember how Jess had at first refused to believe her, then dared her to prove what she claimed. So she had, telling him that her father had gone down to Hidalgo to supervise a transport of illegal workers. She'd said she was ashamed of him and wished he could be stopped.

Jess left soon after. A few hours later, she learned that her father and several other men had been arrested in a shoot-out with border patrolmen who'd sprung a trap for them.

"That was my fault," Andy said to the haunted image of herself she faced in the hotel room mirror. The tapes in her mind whirred on, relentlessly.

An officer had been killed during the bust. Her father stood trial and was sentenced to twenty years. Though it was never officially made public, rumor got out that the man called Jess was really a federal agent, acting undercover to bust those responsible for importing illegal laborers.

Jess had disappeared. There was no one else to stand up for her. Her father blamed her for his arrest. Disowned her publicly in the courtroom after his sentence was passed. Though she learned at his trial that he had been in trouble with the law before—he had just been released from prison when he'd demanded her from her grandmother five years earlier—many of the locals took her father's side. While they couldn't condone what he'd done, they didn't hesitate to find fault in what she'd done. She could still hear their scornful taunts and jeers, calling her trash and worse, a betrayer of her own kin.

"Stop this!" Andy clamped her hands over her ears as if the sounds and sights were coming to her from some outside source. It was useless. They were all in her head.

She'd felt dirty and ashamed of herself. She was stuck in one foster home after another because her grandmother had passed away the previous spring. She was utterly and completely alone. Those foster parents who tried to help her were rebuffed. Rage became her only defense against a world that did not understand her or even want to try. If she'd had the courage she might have tried to commit suicide. But life, miserable as hers had become, had a way of demanding survival. So that's what she'd done—survived—but just barely.

Once she turned eighteen and was finally on her own, she had found her way to Port Isabel where she was hired as a waitress in a local bar. She couldn't actually deliver beer to the table because she wasn't twenty-one but she could take orders and she'd looked awfully good in the hot pants and go-go boots the waitresses wore. Cowboys couldn't get enough of staring and joking and pleading for dates. But she knew her soul mates. They were the men who drank a lot even by Texas standards. They were the wildcatters and the offshore drillers.

Those men worked for weeks at a time on the big rigs. When they came ashore it was with two needs— to romance the local talent and drink their paychecks. Young, brawny and full of themselves, they had alley cat morals and hair-trigger tempers. There'd be at least one brawl a night in the parking lot on the weekend. She always sided with the winner. They didn't care that she'd turned her old man in to the Feds. They rather liked the notoriety that gave her. So she learned to talk tough and act tougher. She made certain she never got cornered but she'd endured the groping most of the waitresses found demeaning. She had just laughed and said it was good for tips. There was a rough kind of honor among the men whose respect she had earned by being as hard and brassy as they were. No man was allowed to press her too hard. Strangers who got too friendly were dealt with. She occasionally even said yes and went out with one of her boozy defenders. She didn't like sex, avoided it altogether as much as possible.

Andy wrapped a trembling hand over her mouth. Even now, she couldn't quite believe the young woman she was remembering was herself. It seemed another life. It *was* another life. But she knew many people who wouldn't see it that way. She had listened to co-workers tell less shameful secrets about themselves over margaritas during happy hour, only to earn rolled eyes and smirks in the hallways for days afterwards.

No one would understand how much pain there had been inside her then. She didn't care that she was earning the reputation that had been forced on her. She had never liked herself very much. After her father's arrest, it wasn't much of a leap to loathing. That lack of self-interest ended up costing her the last thing she had left, her freedom.

Andy went to the window and pulled open the sheers against the open drapes. Below her and a few blocks away Puget Sound gleamed like a giant snail track, as it cut north and west away from downtown. She had come a long way. But was it far enough?

One night she had been drinking, a rare indulgence for her but she'd just learned that her father's year-long bid for a retrial had been denied. Somehow that seemed her fault as well.

Two customers had offered to drive her home. They were semiregulars but no one she had ever dated. When they asked her to sit behind the wheel of the car with the engine running while they got a six-pack at a convenience store, she had happily obliged. She had heard the alarm go off, had seen them come running out. They'd jumped in and told her to floor it, the store was being robbed. She had been too drunk to realize that they were the robbers. The police had explained it to her in great detail after they were arrested half an hour later in another bar.

Andy turned her back on the Seattle morning. She had spent three months in a woman's jail and then four years on probation. The judge told her she was lucky—her companions had been gentlemanly enough to swear she wasn't in on the robbery—but that she must still pay the consequences of keeping bad company and using poor judgment.

She had left Cameron County the day her parole was up, intent on burying Andrea Trask and everything she stood for. She wanted a new life, a different life, one that didn't have a criminal record attached to it.

She had gone north, to Dallas. There she met Eric Connors and he had helped make that transformation possible. For two years she had been someone else. Using her grandmother's maiden name, she became Andy Uchello. This was someone she liked, the person Victor Mondragon had made love to hours earlier.

She thought about the parallels between her story and Victor's. Was it possible that he would understand her, how ashamed she was of her past and her father's? He'd had a good strong family to stand by him, who saw the good in him and saved him from himself. No one had helped her.

She began twisting the gold chain-link watchband round and round her slender wrist. She couldn't bear the thought of seeing the disillusionment in his eyes when he learned the truth, that she had a record and had committed other crimes since, using forged documents and lying about her past in order to get a job. She would rather die. Or leave him before he found out.

The knock on her door was a relief. She glanced at her watch. Albright was early. He must be more anxious than he had seemed over the phone.

She walked as casually as she could to the door, peeked through the spy hole and then slid back the bolt and chain. "Hello, Les."

She saw his gaze dip and then rise in happy surprise. Men were pretty much the same. A short red dress usually brightened their expectations. She wanted him as much on her side as possible. "Hello, Ms. Uchello. Are you expecting someone?"

Andy just smiled. "Come in. My grandmother always said a lady never entertains a gentleman in the doorway."

As he moved past her he chuckled and said, "What would she think of you entertaining in your hotel room?"

Andy's smile widened a fraction. "It would never have occurred to her."

He walked through the room, taking note of her packed bag and then the made bed. "This is a different setup from last time. More cozy."

"Last time I had a little extra cash to burn. This time I'm on the company payroll."

He grinned as he sat in an armchair. "You're a woman who likes nice things."

"Who doesn't?"

He glanced at his watch. She couldn't miss noticing it was expensive. "You could afford many nice things on what I'd pay you."

"No." She didn't try to be polite, to hustle him. She wanted him out of her life. "I told you once before I don't like pushy men." She eyed his chair to make a point. She was still standing. "You used up your second chance at the airport in Dallas. Now, if you don't mind, I have a plane to catch. Let's get this over with."

Her tone of voice withered his smile, as it was meant to. "I can see I've handled things badly with you. But," he stood up and shrugged, rallying his charm, "it's sometimes hard to tell with women. Some say no when they mean yes."

"I never, ever make that particular mistake," Andy answered icily. She reached for her purse and then the handle of her bag. "Your merchandise, or whatever it is, is in the hotel vault. Shall we get it?"

Albright's expression hardened. "You think you're one tough woman. What if I just walked out of here and left it to my client to collect from you?"

"I'd tell them what I'm telling you. It's in the hotel vault. I don't intend to touch it again. It's theirs or yours for the asking. But I wonder what they'd think about you leaving it in the hands of an obvious incompetent like me?"

His lids flickered. "You seemed to have thought of everything."

"I hope so." She felt the heat of her anger register in her eyes. "I don't ever want to see you again. Got it?"

"I don't suppose I have to tell you to keep this transaction of ours to yourself?"

"It would jeopardize my job," she said in clipped tones.

"Right." His gaze hardened and she saw once again the shark behind the custom tailoring. "Let me." He took her bag.

They didn't speak on the elevator ride down. Once again she had the feeling he thought he had said and done all he needed to where she was concerned. Now that it was over, his mind was elsewhere. Their transaction was a mere detail to be seen to.

The retrieval at the cashier's desk was simple because she had called ahead to arrange it.

When the cashier held out the envelope to her, she merely stepped aside for Albright to take it. After she signed for it, she turned to see that Albright had opened it.

He smiled as he pulled out the contents and then returned them to the envelope. Finally he looked at her and smiled. "Sorry we couldn't do business, Ms. Uchello. Still, I'll be in touch, just in case you ever change your mind."

"I won't."

This time her slam-dunk answer didn't seem to faze him. The smile remained. "That's what they all say, at first. But the idea of the cash grows on you." He took several hundred-dollar bills from his inside pocket and tucked them into the pocket on her purse.

"Just to show you that there are no hard feelings, and what you'll be missing. If that doesn't convince you, you should have a little chat with your friend, Eric."

"What are you talking about?" Andy demanded.

Albright shook his head. "Come on. My client waited in this lobby for hours. You hadn't shown up when he left at 3:00 a.m. In my book that translates to you being with a man. Eric couldn't resist calling you, for old time's sake. Right?"

"Right." The words came automatically to Andy's lips. *Eric was alive?*

The room narrowed to the width of a pinprick then widened explosively to blinding clarity. It didn't seem possible. It wasn't—

"Nice doing business with you, Ms. Uchello." She heard Albright's final words above the roaring in her ears. He gave her a mock salute and sauntered across the lobby and out the door.

Andy clutched the back of the nearest lobby lounge chair, telling herself to breathe before she passed out. That would not be wise, especially since she was supposed to duck immediately out of sight. But she couldn't move, couldn't think, couldn't do anything but reel with surprise and disbelief, and the horrible suspicion that Albright was telling the truth. Eric Connors was alive!

What happened then came as a shock, even though she'd known what to expect.

Through the glass doors she watched as Victor stepped out of nowhere to intercept Albright on the curbside as he was about to enter a cab. She saw Victor flash his badge and Albright's jerk of surprise. Then a second man joined them on Albright's free side. Victor waved the cab on. A few seconds later another official-looking vehicle pulled up to the curb and the three men entered the backseat together. It happened so quickly most of the lobby's inhabitants didn't seem to notice anything was going on. Only the doorman had signaled a bellman, who had rushed in to tell the concierge.

Andy turned away, her mind a blank until she heard one of the desk clerks ask her, "What was that all about?"

She gave him an incredulous glance. "I have no idea." The lie sounded convincing. She wished it were true. "Now I'd like to check out."

ERIC WAS ALIVE in Seattle. Andy handled that thought as gingerly as a hot potato throughout her bus trip to the airport. It made a strange kind of sense. His body had not been found because there was no body to find. Which led to the next question: if Eric had survived the wreck, why hadn't he contacted her? She considered several possibilities, the most outlandish being that he had wandered aimlessly about after the accident, a victim of amnesia. Movie plots were full of such intrigues, but real life was a different story. Eric was in Seattle—awfully far to wander.

Albright knew Eric. Knew him well enough to know she and Eric had once been lovers. That could mean Eric was involved with Albright. If so, then it didn't require much of a leap to suspect that Eric had probably also been an illegal courier. There was only one way to find out why Eric had faked his death, or run away, or whatever it was he had done. She had to find him and ask him.

If Eric was tied up with Albright then he could be in trouble. She didn't want to lead Victor to him. She owed him too much to point the Feds in his direction without a hearing. But she herself had to know the truth. She thought of the five one-hundred-dollar bills Albright had stuck in her purse. Eric had always been impressed by easy money. She had dropped the tainted money in a church collection box near the hotel before catching a cab to the airport.

As she sat in the terminal, she continually looked right and left. She was only mildly surprised to see Victor coming toward her as her flight was called. He was a smart man. When he'd discovered she had checked out he knew where to find her.

She stood up, braced herself for angry words. Yet his expression reflected only anxious concern. He didn't stop when he reached her but walked right up against her and embraced her, pulling her so close she could hardly breathe.

"We've done it!" he said, jubilant. He pushed her back to arm's length but he did not release her. The smile on his face was heartbreaking. "So, where are you going?"

"Home." Andy smiled back at him, searching his face for the tiny details that would keep the memory of him fresh for a long time.

He frowned, his black brows swooping low over his golden eyes. "Why? Tomorrow's Saturday. You don't need to be back in Dallas until Monday." He pulled her closer. "Stay with me. I'll make it worth your while."

His slow grin was as effective as his most seductive kiss. She felt it low down and that made what she had to say so much more difficult. "I can't." She glanced away, toward the gate. "I need time to think. It's all been too much, you know?"

Victor's smile dimmed. "What about last night?"

Andy touched his cheek. "It was the most...the best night of my life. But, it's all happened too fast. We each need time."

"I don't!"

"I do."

"I see." He looked suddenly very uncomfortable, an emotional state of which she had thought he was incapable. "If this is about that stupid blunder I made last night when I told you—"

"No, Victor." Oh God! She didn't want him to castigate himself for her sake—not when she was withholding so many more horrible things about herself. "It's not about anything but me. You hardly know me. I'm not good at letting people close."

"You let me in pretty close last night," he drawled. "More than once."

"I don't do intimacy well." She saw his eyes light up in new challenge. "Look, don't make this any harder than it has to be, okay? I want a few days to think about things. Besides, Albright should be occupying your time and attention." She grinned at him. "You got him, Victor. After all this time. You got him dead to rights."

"Maybe."

His hesitation drained the blood from her face. "Don't look like that," he admonished her. "You're perfectly safe. He didn't even suspect we were on to him until we picked him up. Now he's busy trying to get in touch with a lawyer. He had the stolen specifications for a new microchip in his pocket. They were taken from a firm in Boston last week. You're home free."

"You mean you hope so."

Victor nodded. "He's under arrest. Of course, this new wrinkle has brought the FBI into it. They don't intend to give him the chance to do much of anything but rot in prison. If we can indict him on this one, we'll get him on the rest. He or someone he deals with murdered one of my men last spring. We want him bad."

Andy stared at him. "Albright murders people?"

Victor hesitated. Now that he'd held her in his arms he knew the time had come to tip his hand. "I wanted to tell you this before but it didn't seem wise. Now it doesn't matter. We think Eric Connors once worked for Albright."

"Eric?" Andy wondered if her face registered the right amount of shock, or if her ability to be surprised had been damaged these past few days by overuse. She must have revealed some distress for he quickly steered her to a seat and sat down beside her, so close his thigh pressed hers.

"There's more and I can't explain it all but we had just tagged Eric as a possible courier for Albright when he disappeared last winter." He squeezed her hand tight. "Andy, we believe Eric was murdered." He went on quickly, wanting to get it over. "His body was probably disposed of somewhere else and his car ditched in the lake to make his disappearance seem the result of the accident. That's why the police didn't find a body. There wasn't one."

"I see." Andy kept her head down but her mind was in fifth gear. Victor had known about Eric's accident! Had known long before they ever met. "Is that why you assumed I was guilty of working for Albright, because Eric and I were once lovers?"

"No, Andy." Victor tried to put his arm about her shoulders but she shrank away. He abandoned the gesture. "We never even knew he had a live-in girl-friend. We'd just picked up Connors' trail when he disappeared. After that, there was no reason to check into his life."

Andy glanced up. "Why do you keep saying disappeared? You just said you thought he was murdered."

"We do. But there's no proof. It's a working assumption."

"Until the body shows up?"

He nodded. "I'm sorry to lay all this on you here and now but I want you to know that I trust you."

She searched his face. "Do you?"

He didn't lie. "I'm trying, Andy. Just as I want you to trust me."

"I do." In his act of kindness he had only succeeded in making her even more miserable than she had been minutes before. She thought she would cry, except she never cried. "I want to know it's real," she began slowly. "I don't want my feelings for you to be a reaction to the fact that I've been repeatedly frightened this week and you make an awfully good protection device."

He grinned again. "Fair enough. I do have to get back to police headquarters. Now that Albright's been arrested, it's out of our hands. From here on out, everything goes through the attorney general's office. I don't know which jurisdiction will get the case, Seattle or Chicago, Albright's base of operation. Give me a few days to clear things up. Then I'll be back in Dallas." He bent forward and quickly kissed her, as if he thought she would protest. "I'll call you. Okay?"

Andy nodded. "Okay." She popped up from her seat. "You've got to go." She pulled him to his feet and then shoved him away as he tried to kiss her again.

"I hate teary goodbyes," she said in apology. "I'm not good at—"

"Intimacy," he finished for her. "We've got to work on that. Intimacy is one of my favorite things." He smiled but he looked bewildered and hurt, and just a little vulnerable, as if she were taking away some part of him in going. "You look after yourself. The worst is over."

Andy watched him until he was out of sight and then she sat and waited while the flight to Dallas boarded, after which she turned from the gate and headed for the exit.

She wasn't going anywhere until she found Eric.

Victor stepped out of hiding after she passed him and followed her. He hadn't liked spying on her, but, despite his emotional involvement with her, his investigative instincts were still in full working order. He had a feeling she'd been lying to him.

The latest fact sheet on her had come up on his computer the moment he had touched down in Seattle. "Andrea Uchello" was an illegal alias. Her real name was Andrea Trask and her past included a conviction for robbery. A felony.

Victor shook his head. He'd read it twice before the information sank in. Even then, he had been prepared to accept some sort of explanation for her changing her identity and lying about her past. He had followed her all day through Seattle. When he'd decided to confront her on the street, he had been prepared to tell her what he'd learned. But she'd looked so frightened and then so utterly glad to see him. After the first kiss there was no going back. It was inevitable they make love, inevitable and natural, and oh, so dangerous.

Afterward, he had given her a chance to confess, offering his own past as an incentive. She had ducked. That might have been because she was ashamed—or because she was in so deep with Albright that she couldn't afford to trust him with any information that would make him doubt her honesty.

That was too damn bad, Victor thought in disgust and frustration as he sped up to see which way she went when she exited the building. Because he had doubted her, even as she had lain in his arms. The feelings between them only complicated his duty. If she'd confided in him, he would have done everything he could to help her, even if she was working for Albright. But she didn't trust him and for that reason, he couldn't trust himself where she was concerned. So far, his mistrust hadn't steered him wrong. Damn.

Victor paused inside the doorway, watching with bitter regret as her slim figure retreated. He was falling in love, falling hard, but he wasn't a fool.

She had forced him to be a lawman first and a lover second. Whatever he caught her doing now, he would have to act on.

The airport was busy. She had to wait at the cabstand for several minutes before her turn came. It made it easy for him to call in his backup. As he got into the front passenger side, he pointed to the taxi pulling away with Andrea Trask inside. "Follow them, at a distance," he told his driver.

Victor jerked his tie loose and rolled down his window. It was a pleasant seventy-five degrees outside but he felt as if he were in a sauna. The conflict between duty and desire was killing him. But he was going to do his job, even if it broke his heart.

Chapter Eleven

Andy looked up as the waitress rapped sharply on the glass panel of the old-fashioned phone booth. Annoyed, she opened the door a fraction.

"Your lunch is ready," the woman said.

"I'll be there in just a minute." Before the waitress could say more, Andy pushed the door shut and dropped another quarter into the pay phone. She ran a finger quickly down the listings of the phone book open on her lap and then punched in the number.

"Hello! Can I speak to Eric? Eric Connors?" she asked in her broadest Texas drawl. "Are you sure? I'm his cousin from Abilene. I just got into town. I heard he was living here and I just wanted to say hello. Oh well, I'm so sorry to disturb you. That's very kind of you. Thanks a bunch anyway. And have a nice day, you hear?"

Without wasting a moment she flicked the tone switch, fished another quarter from the roll in her lap, put it in the slot and found the next number listed under Connors. She repeated her story twice more before she noticed the waitress standing outside the booth again, a suspicious look in her eye.

Andy took her time gathering her things, telling herself that there was nothing especially suspicious about what she was doing. Still, the first thing the waitress said as she exited the booth was, "You looking for someone?"

Andy smothered the impulse to be rude. "Why yes, I am," she went on in her affected drawl. "My cousin, Eric Connors. He's a cousin of my mama's, second cousin, really. I've just come in from Abilene, only I don't have Eric's address so I can't look up his number." She batted her lashes in a manner that usually revolted her when other women did it. "So, I'm trying them all!"

The waitress's sour gaze didn't alter. "You've been in there half an hour. It's called a public phone because lots of people want to use it."

"I'm sorry," Andy mumbled. She had deliberately chosen this diner down by the docks because she had thought at midafternoon, no one would mind if she tied up the line.

As she slid into the booth where a very greasy hamburger shared the plate with an equally greasy pile of fries, she surveyed the room. It was long and narrow, empty except for two men who sat at the bar drinking coffee. They looked like fishermen in their plaid shirts and deeply tanned faces beneath battered Seattle Mariners baseball caps. Neither of them made a dash for the phone booth she had abandoned.

Andy picked up a French fry between two fingers and, after dabbing it on a paper napkin, began to nibble thoughtfully on it.

In the last two hours she had tried every listing for Connors in the Seattle area phone book. This was her third stop, as she rotated her phone booth use. True, some numbers didn't answer and at other numbers she got an answering machine. Still, she was becoming certain it was a futile attempt.

She reached for her coffee and took a sip, grimacing when the tepid liquid met her lips. She wondered as she set the cup aside how someone found a person who did not want to be found.

She rejected the idea of hiring a private detective. She didn't have much time, or much money. And she couldn't remain in town longer than the weekend. She didn't have a picture of Eric with her, nor did she have any useful suggestions to offer a detective on how to find him. She wasn't about to tell anyone there was the possibility that Eric was working as an illegal courier. That might bring the police to her door with questions of their own. She had thought of hanging out at the airport on the slender hope Eric was about to depart or return from a job. Fridays were often the busiest courier days. But which terminal, and for how long? With Albright under arrest, the whole operation might have gone momentarily underground.

Andy took the top off her hamburger and stuck her fork into the meat, breaking off a small mouthful. She needed a new strategy. However long the odds—and they were extreme—she had to find Eric.

"You aren't very hungry."

Andy had noticed the waitress hovering nearby. The woman's scrutiny reminded her of the days when, as strangers in a new town, she and her father were treated as deadbeats who might run out on a check if not monitored. She pushed down the old feelings, wondering if they would ever entirely leave her. She had a role to play.

She sketched a smile for the woman. "I guess I'm just worried on account of my mama being so adamant that I look up her baby cousin. I just got to find him." Andy's eyes lit up. "Where would a person go who wanted to hear some live music—the real Seattle sound?"

The woman screwed up her face. "You mean like that grunge music? Couldn't tell you. As far as I'm concerned, grunge is just another name for dirt. Now you want to hear good music, you get yourself tickets to Harry Connick, Jr. He's in town tomorrow."

The waitress slapped the check on the tabletop and waited until Andy had taken out her wallet and paid. Only when the money was in her hand did she smile. "Hope you find your cousin, hon."

"Thanks."

Andy left the waterfront diner with one last lead. The man she thought she had recognized as Eric yesterday might, after all, have been him. He had been dressed in a business suit, looked like someone who was leaving his office at the end of the day... maybe a courier agency. She had surreptitiously torn out the listing of delivery agencies in the yellow pages before returning the phone book to its place. Now she needed a city map. She would find the exact corner where she had seen him and then map out the courier agencies to see if any of them were located within a few blocks of that corner.

Half an hour later, she sat in the park near Pike Place Market with a tourist map highlighting the city's top attractions unfolded on her lap. It was good enough to use to locate downtown streets. After eliminating what seemed to be small-time operations and obvious local delivery services, she was left with a dozen possibilities. She painstakingly marked with a red pen the location of each on the map. Five fell within a three-block radius of the corner where, the day before, she had glimpsed the man who resembled Eric.

Andy lifted her head and gazed at the city. It was a needle-in-a-haystack approach but she didn't have any better ideas. She had an hour to kill before she could reasonably begin hanging out on the street corner in hopes of catching sight of him in the rush-hour crowd... if she was right about yesterday.

No, she wouldn't allow herself to consider the possibility that she was wrong. That would eliminate her last lead, however shaky it was. She must concentrate on what to do if she found him. How would she approach him, what would she say?

She picked up the list of names and numbers she had scribbled down as she made calls. "This is useless," she murmured and tossed it in a nearby wastebasket.

She glanced over toward the crafts area where a woodworker had been busy burning a customer's name into a desk plate. As he held it up, the customer said in dismay, "Oh, no! It's supposed to be Russell James not James Russell."

Andy smiled. Some names were easily confused. Eric had liked to switch his name around and mimic foreign accents to charm and tease the unsuspecting, from clients to service people to strangers in a dance club....

"How could I have forgotten?" Andy whispered to herself. With hands that shook she took a sheet of paper from her purse and began writing down the names Eric had used, to her knowledge. Most often they had been a playful blend of his and hers. *Andrew Connors. Erico Uchello. Connor Andrews. Andre Erickson.*

She stuffed her map and notes into a shopping bag and hurried toward the nearest phone booth and directory.

Five minutes later she was staring at the name Andre Erickson in the residential pages. She copied the address then dropped a quarter in the phone and dialed.

After three rings, the answering machine clicked on. The sound of Eric Connors' voice on the taped message was so intimately familiar her knees nearly buckled.

"HELLO, ERIC."

Eric looked surprised but not shocked to see her when he answered his door at 8:30 that evening. It took only a second for him to recover. He flung wide the door. "Andrea! How wonderful to see you!"

He swept her up in an embrace he clearly meant to be loverlike. Andy shoved her purse between them just before their bodies met.

He didn't appear to notice her lack of warmth as he said, "However did you find me?"

"Not with Les Albright's help, if you're wondering," she replied, backing out of his embrace. "You're in the phone book, Mr. *Andre Erickson.*"

He smiled. "You remembered that old trick. Clever girl."

She glanced past him into the spacious hallway of his town house. His address had been listed in the Queen Anne area of Seattle, one of the city's most desirable neighborhoods...and most expensive.

"Aren't you going to invite me in, for old time's sake?"

He swept a hand for her to pass into the entry hall. "You've changed, Andrea," he said as he followed her into his living room with its angular, soaring ceiling.

When she turned abruptly to face him, he nodded in approval. "Red is definitely your color. You never wore it before but the boldness suits you."

"I'm glad you think boldness suits me," Andy answered.

Her glance took in the architectural drama of floor-to-ceiling windows, artful arrangement of objects from places like Mexico and the Far East, and stark, expensive furnishings. When she turned to look at him she was smiling. "You always did have wonderful taste. It looks like now you can afford to indulge it."

"Yes." He smiled and propped an elbow on the nearby mantel. The pose seemed casual, unstudied. She knew it was anything but. He looked newer, more fit, shinier than when she had known him. The fist at his chin invited the eye to admire his clean-cut features and the sheen of his newly highlighted hair. The stretch of his arm called attention to his lean body. Eric's pose was about as unrehearsed as the cover photo on *GQ*. He'd always said presentation was everything. The room was a mere prop for the man.

"So, why did you go to all that trouble to look me up?" he said pleasantly when she continued to stare at him.

"Forgive me," she said coolly. "I'm just admiring the view. You're remarkably well-preserved, for a corpse."

He was fair enough to blush. "I know how it must look." He managed to shrug and toss his head at the same time, a gesture only Latino dancers and classically trained actors could get away with...and Eric. "You're right. I ran out on you. But that was only because I was into something new, something big and I knew how you felt about bending rules."

Andy did some fast calculation. Obviously he thought she knew more about his scam than she did. "You mean breaking the law."

"Yeah. You were green for days after I forged those papers that got you that job with Zane Couriers, remember?" He grinned. The smile that had once been irresistible to her now looked a little forced. Like Albright's.

"I was afraid of being found out," she said slowly, thinking of the bewildered hurt on Victor's face when she'd told him she needed time to think about things. Now that she'd found Eric alive, there were more secrets than ever to keep them apart. "I don't like lying to people."

"Comes with dinner. People expect it."

"So you always said." She paused then let her first feelings of anger show. "You dirty son-of-a—you let me believe you were dead."

"Yeah." He dipped his head and moved slowly away from the mantel. He ran a hand through his hair then grinned sheepishly. "I've missed you."

"Right."

"No, really." He took two steps toward her. "I wanted to tell you but, honestly, it wasn't my shot to call."

"Whose was it? Albright's?"

He blinked. "Yeah. How'd you get mixed up with him?"

"We bumped into one another on a plane. But you were about to explain why you've let me believe you were dead for seven long, awful months."

She was only half surprised that her words perked him up. "Did you really miss me?" he asked. She put up a hand in a gesture like a policewoman stopping traffic as he tried to approach her.

"I don't blame you for being angry," he said. "Can't really. It was just that I needed a quick out. I owed a couple of collection services money I couldn't pay back right then. Albright had promised me a sweet spot in his business if I would relocate to Seattle. So I ditched the car, making it seem like I'd had an accident. The new name was sort of insurance against being found. Still, I thought you'd guess I was up to something when a body didn't float to the top." He looked injured that she hadn't figured it out before. "You're smart enough to have found me now."

Incredulous, Andy stared at him. She might have laughed if it hadn't hurt so much. He was blaming her for not knowing he wasn't dead! It had been nothing more than a game to him, another of his pranks. One big laugh. He felt no remorse for the pain and suffering she had endured, thinking him dead. Why hadn't she seen it before? Keisha was right. Eric always put himself first.

"I know what you're thinking, Andy, that I should have brought you along, hooked you up. But this isn't the business for you."

"Why? It certainly seems to be doing all right by you."

He shrugged again. This time it was a gesture of annoyance. "That's because I know how to handle myself with people like Albright. You don't. Stay away from him, Andy. He'll only cause you grief."

"Unlike you?" She glanced deliberately around the room again. "There must be an awful lot of money involved in this setup."

His gaze finally met hers squarely. "You don't even want to know."

How many times had she heard that phrase when they had lived together? In those days she thought it meant he was protecting her from something that could harm or alarm her. Now, she realized, he had probably been protecting himself. She felt a little sick. Had she been that naive, or so desperate that she'd have believed anything to keep him on her side?

She had one more button to push. "Mr. Zane has offered me a job here in Seattle."

His eyes widened in undisguised alarm. "You're kidding? You're not going to take it, are you?"

He must have seen the fury that leaped into her expression because he switched tactics yet again. "I mean it's a nice town but it rains—a lot. And it's too cool most of the year to enjoy the beaches. You're a long way from anywhere else."

She'd heard all she needed to know. He didn't want her in Seattle. "Why would Albright have someone ransack my apartment?"

Eric chuckled for the first time. "He didn't. *I* did."

"You!" Again she was taken completely by surprise. "Why?"

"To warn you off. Albright came to town talking about this woman he had met on a plane, said he tried to recruit her when he found out she worked for the same courier service in Dallas I once had." He wasn't looking at her and she could almost see the wheels turning in his head. He was constructing his story as he went along. She didn't doubt that vital bits of information were being edited out. "I told him I knew you and that you weren't right for the job." He glanced at her. "You were too honest."

"Thanks for the vote of confidence."

"No, I mean it. But Albright said he was going to pursue you anyway. I think he's got the hots for you. I got on the first plane and went to Dallas. I wanted to talk to you but how would it have looked if I'd just knocked on your door and said, 'Hi, Andy. Remember me?'"

"It would have made more sense than what you did."

His brows dipped in annoyance. "I didn't want Albright to know I'd seen you."

She didn't bother to ask why. She knew he'd only lie. "So how was I supposed to connect your trashing my apartment with not working for Albright?"

He shrugged, a habit that was beginning to bug her to no end. "I just wanted to spook you. I thought you would think Albright had done it, and refuse to have anything to do with him."

It didn't make sense but it was just the sort of perverted logic Eric might have applied to the situation. After all, this was a man who had faked his death in order to cheat his creditors. She studied him carefully, and noticed for the first time the white square bandage that covered the lower half of his left palm. The thief had tripped leaving her apartment and left a bloody palm print on the stairwell. "Did you decide to smash my face before or after you'd trashed the apartment?"

"Jesus! I didn't mean to hurt you. You startled me. I thought when you didn't show by 8:00 that you were out of town. I didn't do any real damage. The stereo wasn't touched." He seemed almost proud of his thoughtfulness. "I was just finishing up when you walked in. I had to scare you so you wouldn't look up and recognize me."

"With a gun?"

He looked sheepish as he pulled a pen out of his breast pocket. "It was only the tip of my twenty-four-karat gold pen."

"You bastard!"

"Right, right." He put up both hands. "Let's not get emotional here."

But she was feeling very emotional. She wanted nothing more than to blow him out of the water. "Albright's been arrested."

"What?" He squawked the word. Bull's-eye!

"I saw it happen right outside my hotel." She kept her voice low, her tone matter-of-fact. "He had just picked up the package I had refused to deliver for him when, out of nowhere, these men in suits grabbed him by both arms and hustled him away. I heard the concierge explaining to a startled guest that they were policemen."

For the first time he looked really worried. "What did they want?"

"Why don't you tell me?" It occurred to her again that Albright's arrest could mean big trouble for Eric, unless she protected him. But the old habit of loyalty was fading fast.

He began pacing. "You're sure you're okay?" Before she could reply he added, "I mean, you're sure you aren't being followed or anything?"

Andy's last kind impulse toward him died. "Good-bye, Eric." She turned and walked toward the door.

"Wait." He came running after her and put a hand on her arm to halt her. "Wait, Andy. Let's talk a bit more."

Andy searched his boyishly handsome face with a detachment that surprised even her. "How deep are you in?"

His expression shuttered over.

"That deep? So, maybe you'd better disappear again."

He nodded, taking her sarcasm for advice. "Right, for a while." He then looked at her accusingly. "Why couldn't you leave well enough alone?"

Andy tried to keep the hurt inside her from showing. "That's what I'll be asking myself for a long time."

"You won't tell anybody you've seen me?"

"What would I say? I ran into Eric in Seattle and for a dead man he looked great?"

Smiling in relief, he couldn't keep from trying to draw her close one last time. "I *have* missed you. That's why I couldn't resist snatching that Mardi Gras photo of us." His hands began to massage her upper arms. "How 'bout it, for old time's sake?"

She leaned in just enough to make him think she was going to kiss him and said in her huskiest voice, "Drop dead!" She pulled abruptly away.

"Andy, be careful," he said, trailing after her toward the door. "Albright has friends—business partners. With the help of the kind of lawyers he can afford, he could be back on the street in days. You'd better play dumb about everything if the police come calling. Understand? And you never saw me, okay?"

Andy pulled his own door shut in his face.

Once back on the street, she breathed deeply of the cool, tangy night air. Nothing about the last ten hours seemed real. Last night she had been deliriously happy, she was falling in love . . . now she was in more of a mess than ever. And farther away than ever from being able to make Victor proud of her.

She knew Eric was alive. She knew he was involved with Albright. That was enough to get him arrested. But could she do it, turn him in? And how would that look to a man like Victor? Would he think she was doing her patriotic duty, or ratting on a former lover? She didn't know and until she figured it out, she didn't want to talk to or see Victor Mondragon. She was going to lose him, she just knew it!

For hours she had been battling dozens of thoughts, each more dismal and depressing than the last. Now she knew that Eric, the man she had once thought the world of, was a cheat, a liar, a fraud and a coward all rolled up into one. Could she pick them, or what?

"Men! I hate them!" she wailed into the night and then rushed down the street in the direction of the rental car she had deliberately parked on the next block.

"FOLLOW HER?"

"What else?" Victor answered as the man behind the wheel turned the key in the ignition.

They had been parked across the street, waiting for her to exit the house. Victor checked his watch. She'd been in there exactly ten minutes. He reached for the unopened pack of cigarettes in his breast pocket.

"I didn't know you smoked."

"I don't," Victor answered as he punched in the cigarette lighter. "Gave it up months ago."

His driver smiled. "This job does that to people."

"Right." It had been exactly nine hours and twenty minutes since he had followed Andy out of the airport. During that time he had watched her spend hours in phone booths making call after call. He knew she was trying to locate someone. But who? He imagined she had been calling Albright's connections. Then he retrieved a crumpled slip of paper with the name Connors scribbled on it, which Andy had dropped into a park wastebasket.

Suddenly her actions took on a whole new meaning. That's when he'd bought his first pack of cigarettes in months.

She had rented a car and then she'd gone sightseeing, seemingly wasting time, as if she were waiting for something or someone. Then, she'd driven out here.

The cellophane made rattling noises as he opened his pack and pulled one out.

The phone buzzed.

Victor paused as he was about to light the cigarette and picked up the receiver. "So, did you get a name for this address?" He printed rapidly on his pad the name Andre Erickson.

Andre. Andy. Andy Erickson. Andy and Eric.

He muttered a four-letter word. She'd played him for a first-class fool, all the way.

He tossed his unlit cigarette out the window.

"I DON'T CARE if you're overbooked by a dozen. I must get on this flight!"

Andy ignored the stares of the other passengers waiting at the gate. She wasn't going to spend one more second in Seattle.

"As I've said, all I have is a no-show seat in first class," the attendant behind the counter explained in a patient if weary voice, "and that won't be officially available until after our final call."

"I'll take it."

"There will be an extra charge," the flight attendant cautioned her.

Andy leaned over the counter and said in a low angry voice, "I don't care!"

Once aboard the plane, Andy settled into her seat, pulled a sleeper's blindfold from her bag and slipped it into place, ignoring the attractive man seated next to her. He could have been Mel Gibson and it wouldn't have mattered. She didn't want to look at, speak to, or deal with another handsome man as long as she lived!

Chapter Twelve

As they stepped off the racquetball court and headed for the showers, both women were breathing hard. "Whose head in particular were you trying to smash back there?" Keisha Jackson asked.

Andy swung her racket at an imaginary image of Eric Connors' head. "I don't know what you mean."

"Get over it. Your strokes were coming so hard and fast even the ball knew the abuse was personal."

Andy swiped the sweat from her forehead with her wristband. "Maybe I was letting off a little steam."

"Well, I hope you got it out of your system." Keisha paused to return the bold look of the two men approaching them. She chuckled when they parted to let the women pass, then went on without missing a beat. "First, you take two personal days at the beginning of the week. Then you come in this morning and tell our best customer where to get off. If I hadn't had the ready story that your nerves were on edge because you'd been burglarized, I don't know if Mr. Lohr would have been so understanding."

"How did you—?" Andy paused. Of course. Keisha's husband would have heard about the incident at police headquarters. "I don't want to talk about it."

"I hear you didn't lose much but that doesn't mean it wasn't scary for you, right?"

Andy blew out her cheeks as the sweat streamed down her flanks. "Can we talk about something else?"

"Okay. How about the fact that you weren't answering your phone all weekend."

Andy rolled her eyes as they stepped into the women's locker room. "I needed time to think." She stripped off her leotard. "I've had a lot on my mind."

Keisha followed suit, but she was more careful not to strain the seams of her new workout clothes. The gym was the one luxury in which she indulged herself. Andy knew her budget didn't permit for many extras, like new leotards. She was most often Keisha's partner on Wednesdays for racquetball.

"I like that color on you," Andy said. "And you've lost that last five pounds, haven't you?"

Keisha beamed and patted her flat stomach. "I sure did. I thought that third pregnancy had sprung me for good."

Andy smiled. "I'm sorry about what happened in the office today. I just don't feel like myself." She glanced away and lifted a foot up on the bench to begin unlacing her shoes. "Also, I owe you an apology. You were right about Eric and I was wrong."

Keisha glanced at her in surprise. "Now, what brought that on?"

Andy kept her head down and she slipped off her shoes and socks. "What you said last week. It made me think. I was blind to a lot of things where Eric was concerned. He was good to me and I'll never forget that, but I think he was up to something when he—died."

"Up to what?"

"Did you ever think maybe Eric was into something illegal?"

Keisha nodded her head once then reached into her locker to retrieve a towel. She bent closer as she added, "Between you and me, I think he was in trouble when he died. A few days after his car was found these goons came to the office looking for him, said he owed them money. They looked like muscle, if you know what I mean. A collection agency on two feet? I think Eric was betting on the ponies over at the Shreveport race tracks."

"Anything else?"

Keisha stepped into her shower shoes and then busily tucked her hair into a purple shower cap.

"Keisha?"

She glanced across at Andy, her dark eyes skeptical. "You know how I feel about gossip. Some kinds can get a person fired and I've got a husband and three kids counting on me having a job."

"So?"

Keisha took her by the arm and dragged her toward the showers. "What do you want to know for? You think somebody messed up your apartment after all these months to get you to pay Eric's old debts?"

"No, nothing like that. In fact, I didn't know he gambled. I guess I didn't want to know too much. I was a fool."

"You were in love."

"No." Andy said it flatly. Now that she'd had the barest hint of what real love could be like, she knew she'd never loved Eric, not by her new understanding of the word. "I was young, foolish and scared and

Eric was kind. I didn't want to look a gift horse in the mouth."

"I also think he was moonlighting," Keisha said as they stood in the aisle of shower stalls. "Something illegal."

Andy wet her lips. "What kind of illegal?"

Keisha shrugged. "I only know once he came into the office on his way out on a trip and left his pouch lying around for anyone to tamper with. I picked it up and opened it to see whose package he was treating so casually. I had no more than read the address when he came flying over and snatched it from me. Said it was personal. I told him if he didn't want his personal business looked into he better keep it out of Zane Courier pouches."

"Did you report him?"

Keisha turned to open the door of an empty stall. "I believe in minding my own business, unless it has to do with my job or somebody I care about. Eric got the message."

Andy grabbed the shower door as Keisha was about to shut it. "Who was the package for?"

Keisha looked at her sourly. "I don't know why I'm telling you this. The address was a bank in the Grand Caymans." She dropped her towel. "Now, if you don't mind?"

Andy shut the door for her.

Ten minutes later they left the climate-controlled interior of the health club for the sweltering ninety-nine-degree temperature of the final Wednesday in August. The waves of heat rolling up from the asphalt made Andy grimace and squint as she fumbled in her bag for her sunglasses.

"Well, excuse me!" she heard Keisha say as she shoved her sunglasses into place. "Who is that fine thing leaning on your bumper?"

Andy rotated her head to the left, half knowing whom to expect. He was lounging against the bumper of her ancient Volvo, arms folded and legs crossed at the ankles. He wore a business suit and tie and a scowl.

"Just someone I met," Andy answered, frowning at Victor because she wasn't at all certain she welcomed her heart's enthusiastic response to sighting him.

Keisha gave her an inquiring look over the tops of her sunglasses. "Well now, Miss 'I'll Be Over Eric Any Day Now.' Looks like you found the cure. I'd say that's one fine time ahead of you this evening."

Keisha raised her hand to wave to Victor before heading off toward her car. "You be careful, Andy," she called cheerfully over her shoulder. "You've heard good-looking men have only one thing on their minds! Hope for your sake it's true!"

Andy approached Victor with all the eagerness of a matador facing a bull without a cape or sword. She had been avoiding his calls ever since she returned to Dallas because she had not yet decided what to do about Eric and the whole mess. She had half hoped Victor would simply give up on her. Her other half was wildly pleased to see him. But why did he have to track her down here, when she was least prepared to deal with him?

She wore white shorts and a camisole top. She hadn't bothered to dry her hair or put on any makeup other than lipstick. She intended to go straight home and stay there, alone. Now she was wishing for a mascara wand, curling iron, her new sundress and sandals so she would look beautiful for this man she couldn't forget.

Victor came to his feet as she neared him but there was no welcome on his face. His fists were shoved into the pockets of his suit pants. His face was slicked by sweat. The scowl on it was enough to bring her up short a few paces shy of friendly distance.

Tall and bronze and glowingly male with the summer breeze flagging his black mane, he looked like an unhappy Aztec god who had come to chastise one of his worshipers. Well, she almost qualified. She did admire him, damn it!

To cover her own mixed feelings about seeing him, her first words weren't friendly. "What are you doing here?"

"You weren't returning my calls. We need to talk." He jerked his head toward the car parked opposite hers.

"I'll drive," she said stubbornly, just to keep what little control she had over the situation.

"Suit yourself." He stepped aside while she unlocked the passenger side of her car and then walked around to open the driver's side. He slid in beside her, saying nothing about the lack of room her old coupe offered his long body.

"Where to?" Andy asked, her hands flexed on the steering wheel.

"Somewhere we can shout and not be disturbed."

Andy smiled in spite of herself. "I know just the place."

Ninfa's off Stemmons Freeway had long been her favorite Mexican restaurant. For Dallas aficionados of true Tex-Mex, Ninfa's had remained one of the few genuine articles. The tamales were authentic. The tortillas were shaped and cooked while customers watched. The decor was bright and festive and slightly tacky, like a Mexican market. The crowd was huge and the noise rambunctious. None of it drowned out the lively mariachi band music. A couple could have one blistering shouting match without drawing a neighbor's eye.

Andy plowed a crisp chip into the chunky homemade salsa without waiting for the beers they had ordered. So far, she and Victor had not said more than two words at a time to each other. Now he was lounging in the high-backed cane-bottomed chair opposite her, watching her with narrowed eyes as his fingers played restlessly on the painted wooden edge of the tabletop.

Her gaze lingered on his fingers before moving away. She had always thought he had good hands, hands she wouldn't mind feeling on her skin again. Now she wished he'd kept them under the table and out of sight so that they wouldn't be able to inspire daydreams she couldn't afford to indulge.

She knew what she had to do but that didn't mean she was eager to get on with it. The answer to her situation had been building in her thoughts for days. The only thing worse than her fear that Victor would learn about her past and the secrets in her present was her dread that, once he did, he would walk away from her. She knew only one way to end the pain. She must push him away first. But not just yet.

She reached for the jalapeño pepper among the various pickled vegetables on the table and bit into it. She had always liked her food hot and her men dangerous. Perhaps it was time she gave up both. Or maybe she just needed tequila. No, she'd end up taking Victor home with her for sure.

"Andy?" When she ignored him, Victor switched seats, moving beside her instead of remaining opposite her. He reached for her hand but she drew away. "You asked me for the weekend. Now it's Wednesday and you won't take my calls or return my messages. What's with you?"

Andy pulled herself together and looked at him, wishing he wasn't so close she could see each individual sooty lash. She had stroked those long lashes with her fingertips in the lazy aftermath of lovemaking. "Remember I said I wanted time to think? Well, I thought."

Her gaze drifted south of his face to the brown hollow of his throat exposed when he'd ditched his tie and opened his collar. "What we had was a good time. A really good time. But it was just one of those things."

"Not for me it wasn't."

"Well, too bad." Her eyes shot up to meet his. Anger had always been her best defense. "It was all smoke and heat and danger and forbidden fun. Now it's over."

"Why?"

She wanted to smack him for the dogged determination in his expression. "Call it a one-night stand." She smirked. "Surely you've had one-night stands?"

"Not like that," he answered with such force that she didn't dare to lie about her own. "And not since I've known better."

She took another chip but he grabbed her hand to keep her from putting it in her mouth. "Andy, talk to me. If you're scared about testifying, you needn't be."

Andy snatched her hand free and stuck the chip in her mouth. She choked, and it wasn't a diverting measure.

By the time she had taken a few sips of water and caught her breath, what dignity she had was gone. She felt stupid and awkward and miserable.

"The case is falling apart," Victor suddenly said without preamble. He leaned forward and braced his forearms on the table. "We need your testimony."

"I asked you to leave me alone," she finally murmured.

He went on, as if he hadn't heard her. "When I say the case is falling apart, I mean the Treasury Department's end has gotten shaky. It's all very complicated but here's the short version. We picked up Albright and now the FBI is saying it should have been their collar because Albright wasn't carrying stolen bills or securities but plans gotten by industrial spying. We didn't have probable cause or jurisdiction. If we can't link him to our ongoing investigation, he may walk."

"But he had stolen documents on him," Andy said in disbelief.

"It wasn't Treasury related, so maybe it's not a legal bust."

Andy sighed. "So what? If I was stopped for a traffic ticket and the officer found cocaine in the glove compartment, are you saying he couldn't arrest me?"

"It depends. The officer would have to show reason for the search, probable cause. If you weren't licensed or the car was stolen or you were drunk, something already illegal, then he could pursue the search. Otherwise..."

"You know Albright had carried illegal stuff before in the suitcase I was asked to pick up."

"Exactly."

As his eyes lit up Andy realized she had backed herself into a corner. "You want me to testify that Albright duped me into carrying for him before?"

Victor nodded and reached for her hand again. This time she didn't argue. "We need you, Andy. I need you, and not because of my case. But you could make a difference."

I could make a difference all right, Andy thought miserably. She had had a lot of time to think these last days. With her past as fodder, a good attorney—and Albright could probably afford the best—would make mincemeat of her as a reliable state's witness. That would make Victor seem a fool before his superiors and ruin everything. "I can't."

"Why not?"

Andy hung her head, more ashamed than she had been in a long time. "I—I'm not a good witness. I'll ruin your case." She shook her head, her feet inching her chair away from the table as if she didn't have enough space to breathe. "You don't want me in the witness box, believe me."

"I know you have a record."

Her head snapped up so quickly she felt a little crack in her neck. He was looking at her with such intensity she felt her cheeks burn and yet she couldn't look away.

He knew. The words kept tolling in her head like the bells of the local mission church near Yard, Texas, which rang slow and mournfully each time a parishioner died. Dear God, no! "You know?"

He nodded slowly, his gaze never leaving her face. "I know you are Andrea Rose Trask. I know you were convicted of a felony in Cameron County court six years ago as an accessory to a robbery.''

Suddenly Andy was calm again, so calm she no longer felt alive. "How long have you known?"

This time his lids flickered. "A while."

"How long, damn you?" She was surprised by the pain that exploded in her fist until she realized she had banged it on the tabletop. Then she noticed the curious glances aimed her way. She had been wrong. Some kinds of raised voices did attract attention, even at Ninfa's.

When her gaze swung back to Victor he said simply, "Before we made love."

"Before." Andy gripped the tabletop to stop her world from reeling. "You bastard," she whispered low. "You used me. What did you think? That I might run out on you before I'd help you set Albright up? So you decided to keep me entertained?" She nearly choked on the rage and embarrassment and pain pressing at the back of her already aching throat.

"You know it wasn't like that." Desperation edged into his voice as he leaned closer. "It just happened. Andy, I didn't mean it to happen without first telling you what I knew."

"Oh?" she said brightly, ignoring the wounded depths of his eyes. Fighting was one of the few things she knew how to do well. "Now I remember, you did start that conversation. It went something like, 'By the way, before I unhook your bra, I think you should know I know you're an ex-con.'" Rage leaked like acid through her words. "Am I right?"

"Don't do this," Victor said, his tone a warning.

But she'd once been accustomed to self-destructive public displays. She stood up, knocking over her chair.

"I hate you!" She turned and hurried blindly for the door.

She didn't look back, didn't really look forward as she headed for the door like a bullet while patrons and waiters scattered to get out of her way.

She hit the first pair of double doors and then the second. She was in the parking lot before she realized she'd left her purse hanging on her chair back. But she couldn't go back, couldn't do anything but heave sobs of pain and fury and writhe with the old humiliation of self-loathing. She stumbled over to her car, folded her arms on the hot metal roof and cried.

Victor followed as quickly as he could, scooping up her purse and pressing a twenty-dollar bill in the hand of the hostess. He knew she couldn't get far without her keys, unless she was so out of control she had flagged down a car and hitched a ride. That thought had him trotting by the time he reached the final doors. He spied her across the parking lot before the doors fully opened.

He didn't try to comfort her, he simply unlocked the driver's side of the car and got in behind the wheel. After a few moments she collected herself and climbed into the passenger side. He fumbled in her purse until he found a packet of tissues. She took a handful and wiped her face. He didn't look at her, didn't speak. She was still sobbing, little hard sounds that lacerated his conscience. He had thought he would find the right time to tell her what he knew. Instead, he'd made the mother of all misjudgments.

He drove to her home, which wasn't far. When he had pulled the car around back he turned to her, his face strained by the need to say the right thing. "I'm sorry, Andy. I'm so damned sorry."

She didn't look at him, only reached for the door handle.

He followed her upstairs. She was moving like a mechanical doll, going through the right motions but not really consciously aware of them.

He unlocked her door, grateful for the burst of air-conditioning that greeted them. The late-afternoon sun slanted through her nearly shut blinds, offering the only light. When she just stopped moving once she was inside the door, he very lightly put his hands on her shoulders. She didn't resist so he gently steered her toward her sofa. "I'll get you some water," he said, sounding like a host instead of an uninvited guest.

He came back from her kitchen with the biggest glass he could find. As he held it out to her he looked into her face. What he saw shocked him.

She looked like a lost child. Gone was all the toughness and bravado that added piquancy to her pretty face. Gone was all the self-confidence of knowing she was a beautiful, sexy woman. Gone were all the complex emotions. Only the fear he had first seen lurking behind her dark eyes remained. That fear filled her face, pinching her nostrils and making caverns of her eyes and dimming her natural and unique beauty.

He sat down very slowly beside her, as close as he dared, and held the glass while she took a few short sips. When she was done, she pushed the glass away with both hands, like a child.

Stricken by remorse, Victor turned his gaze away from her. What on earth had he done to her? He had expected her to be insulted, angry, frightened by his revelation. But she was a fighter. He had expected an in-your-face attack, stonewalling and sarcasm, aggression that would divert him from the truth. Instead, she looked as if he had pulled the plug on her life force.

"I never wanted you to know."

Her quiet, husky voice brought his head swinging around to see that she was looking at him. "Know what, Andy?"

"Not because you're a cop," she continued. "No, that was part of it. All of it, at first. But not later." She swallowed painfully. "You're a decent person. I'm not. I just didn't want you to ever know that about my past."

Victor watched her curl her legs under herself and fold her arms in close, becoming a smaller and smaller ball, as if she were trying to disappear. It broke his heart.

She was ashamed of her past.

It had occurred to him that she might really be an innocent party where Albright was concerned, that the secrets lurking in her eyes were her own to keep. He had wished, needed, wanted it to be true. But it had not been a belief upon which he had operated. He had kept digging because he couldn't afford such faith in her. He had doubted his own intuition about her because she was a stranger, an unknown. It was time that changed. "Won't you tell me what happened to you, Andy?"

At first she was silent, staring inwardly into some place and time he could never really fully know. Then she began to speak.

She talked for a long time, rambled really, about her grandmother and Yard, Texas, and grapefruit orchards, then her father and how she'd hated him from day one. She talked about her life on the road with him, of always being the transients in a society that prized stability and was suspicious of anything not three generations old.

She told the story of her father's arrest and her part in it with great detachment. Victor could guess how much she must have liked and trusted that undercover agent to share her secret with him. He also began to understand why she had disliked him so much in the beginning, another federal agent, and had fought the attraction that was instant and mutual and so unlike what either of them expected. He understood that and much more. In reality she had been alone since she was ten, making herself up as she went along.

What he could not imagine was how sad and frightened that must have made her and what it must have taken to come out of it as well as she had. She had made an innocent mistake that had exploded in her face. The agent should have been disciplined for using a child that way. He had been tempted to step over the line himself, pulled by circumstance and the frustrated need to win. But his only true indiscretion had been of the personal kind, with this woman, an indiscretion of the heart.

He hurt inside for her as she told him about her days in Port Isabel. Though he would never tell her so, her arrest might have been the best thing that could have happened to her. She was headed for destruction. Drugs and prostitution wouldn't have been far behind if something hadn't broken the cycle. Or maybe he was wrong. Maybe she was stronger than that. He would never know. Yet he did now know what she had endured and risen above, and his admiration wasn't diminished by his new knowledge of her, but ex-

panded into a quiet certainty that she was not someone he could walk away from again.

Once he had thought her spoiled and a gold digger.
How wrong he'd been. She was tough because she'd
had to be. She was suspicious because life had taught
her several hard lessons about trust. She was strong
enough to remake herself and start again. He couldn't
condone the method, forging papers to erase her old
life, but he certainly understood the reasons behind it.
And she knew the value of loyalty. Whatever he
thought of the man she knew as Eric Connors, her
actions proved she knew how to be faithful. Now he
wanted all that toughness and loyalty and hard-to-win
trust in his life and he no longer knew if it was possible.

He wondered if she realized how much she was
trusting him with at this very moment. Little by little
she had begun to unwind as she talked, relaxing
against the sofa back. She didn't pull away when he
encouraged her to rest her head on his shoulder. Nor
later, when she talked about the days in prison, did she
stop him from stroking her temple lightly and then her
brow. Finally, she was leaning her weight fully against
him as she lay half curled in his lap. He held her with
one arm about her shoulders and the other across her
waist. She felt small and fragile yet calm now and res-
olute, someone who needed and had earned his protection and respect.

When she finally ran out of words the room was
wrapped in shadows so deep he could no longer see his
feet on the floor. But he didn't move to switch on a
light. In the darkness the world was gone. There was
just the two of them, alone, together as he had wanted
it to be from the first. Now that he knew the truth, he

could help her. He would help her. No matter what her connection to Albright and Eric Connors.

"I love you."

His own words didn't surprise him but they sent a shudder of recognition through him just the same. He did love her. Whether that love would endure depended on things other than his own certainty. Andy stirred against him, her head dipping onto his chest. "Andy, did you hear me? I said—"

Andy cut him off with a hand against his mouth. "Don't. Not now. Later. Maybe."

Victor bent and kissed the crown of her head. "Just so you know where we stand, okay?" He lifted a hand to her face. "Damn, you're freezing. Let's get you a hot bath and then something to eat."

He didn't wait for her to reply but scooped an arm under her hips and shifted her into his lap before he rose with her in his embrace.

"Just what do you think you're doing?"

Her voice! The old Andy's suspicious voice made him smile in the dark as he warily threaded his way through the gloom. "I'm probably about to stumble over something and break my neck," he answered with a smile. "Do you suppose you could direct me to your bedroom?"

Andy shifted in his embrace and then he felt her arms loop about his neck. "I thought white knights knew all about the way to a damsel's bedroom."

Victor dipped his head and found a cheek to kiss. "I'll show you what I know about a lady's bedroom after you've warmed up."

Her arms tightened about his neck and then he felt her lips skimming his cheek toward his mouth as she said, "Show me first, Victor."

"It might be the best way to warm you up, anyway," he agreed pleasantly. But he felt more than desire rise in him as their lips met. It was elation and gratitude. In spite of everything, how badly he had mismanaged the encounter, she was gallant and generous enough to remain honest and uncalculated in her feelings. Such old-fashioned virtues were rare and her gift to him.

They made love tentatively at first, as if each was afraid the other might pull away at the last moment. But the gentleness gradually altered as the need to be part of each other, at least for a while, overwhelmed the wariness of the unknown.

Victor found ways of expressing himself he had never before even known the desire to try. He praised her with words and touches, with sighs and whispers in Spanish, with his hands and lips, with kisses and stroking, and finally with the syncopated union of their bodies and his hoarse cries of pleasure. And she was there with him, all the way, accepting, offering, returning everything he gave. Her cry of fulfillment was the greatest pleasure of all.

"THE BEST NUMBER in the world is two," Andy said as she lay on her stomach in bed beside Victor. He was stretched out on his back with his arms folded behind his head, flagrantly and unapologetically naked. His eyes were half closed but he was watching her fingers move over his skin.

"Two eyes, two nostrils, two cheeks, two lips," she counted as her fingers spider-walked down his face. "Two shoulders, two nipples, two sets of ribs. Ah!

You're ticklish! One navel. Oh, well. Two hips, two—''

"*Cajones,*" Victor supplied as she blushed.

"Right, but only one of these." Her hand stilled over him.

Victor grinned at her. "It's not the quantity, it's the quality that counts, *querida.*"

Andy smiled back at him. A few short hours ago she had thought it was impossible that they would ever be here like this in her bed. Now she realized she had wanted it so badly she couldn't allow herself to hope for it. "I'm not accustomed to having my wishes come true," she said with uncharacteristic candor.

"Then your luck's about to change." Victor lunged up and over her, pushing her flat on the bedding. "Anything you want, anytime you want it, you just call Victor Mondragon. He will take care of his woman."

His smile heated up her middle and she squeezed him gently. "Tell me again how I am 'the star in the dark night of your soul.'"

Victor drew back, his expression suspicious. "You know Spanish?"

"*Sí, señor.* I didn't grow up within spitting distance of the Mexican border for nothing. But, really, your flattery is so poetic. I didn't want to inhibit you by replying in my Tex-Mex."

He rubbed his body over hers. "I don't think much can inhibit me now that we're here like this."

"Wait." Andy stretched her arm out to hold his kiss away. "There are things I have to tell you, Victor. Things about your case."

Victor pushed past her hand and kissed her, hard, easing only into seductive pressure when she acquiesced. "Not now," he said against her mouth when he'd had enough assurance that she wanted this as much as he did. "Let this be for us. We've earned the right to a little happiness. The rest can wait. It sure as hell won't go away."

The sound of her doorbell made Andy jerk away from his descending mouth.

"Who could that be?" she questioned in surprise as she stared out the bedroom doorway.

"Your friend from the health club?" Victor suggested.

Andy shook her head as the bell sounded a second time. "I'd better go see."

Victor held her firmly by the waist. "Why?"

Andy looked at him, one dark brow arched. "This is my house. I get to make the rules."

He released her reluctantly, watching in proprietary pleasure as she slid sleekly from the bed and darted into the bathroom. She returned a moment later, shrugging into a long green silk robe. It trailed seductively behind her as she crossed the room so that he glimpsed one last arousing view of her naked body before she pulled it around herself and tied it.

He lay back with a sigh and shifted his hips to ease his need. He hoped she wouldn't be long. He had just thought of how much he was going to enjoy peeling her inch by inch out of all that emerald silk.

Andy switched on lights as she went, giving her living room a quick sweeping glance to make certain no telltale signs of her visitor were about. She clicked on the outside hallway light and pressed an eye to the peephole. A moment later she was staring through her open door at the last face she expected to see at this time of night.

"Hello, Ms. Uchello. Mind if I come in?"

"Mr. Zane."

Chapter Thirteen

"I hope I'm not disturbing you," Elijah Zane said as he stepped into her tiny hall.

"I was about to go to bed," Andy answered brusquely. She refused to give in to the impulse to draw the neckline of her gown closed even though Zane's gaze had wandered to it as she mentioned bed.

"I've been out of town on business," he said, finally dragging his gaze from the deep V. "Just got back into town. I wouldn't bother you but I need to ask you some questions about company business." He pointed to the sofa in the living room. "Do you mind if I sit down?"

"I suppose not, if it's important," Andy answered. Not wanting to give him any room to interpret her state of undress as an invitation of any kind, she added, "Just let me change."

"I won't be here long enough for that," Zane answered as he gave the room a long, searching look. Then he looked back at her. "Besides, you look just fine."

Andy moved to the single over-stuffed chair in the room and perched on the arm. "You said you have business to discuss."

He sat down and balanced his Stetson on his knee. "That's right. Disturbing facts have come to light in the last few days. Facts about you, Ms. Uchello."

Andy didn't even flinch. She had been through hell once today. Nothing else could touch her. "Well, Mr. Zane? I'm your only audience. Perhaps you'd like to speed this up?"

His brows lowered over his blue-gray eyes. "All right. I've been approached by federal authorities who say you're wanted for questioning about an incident that took place in Seattle last Friday. Since you work for me, they had a few questions to ask me about your employment record. Naturally, I told them what little I know."

Andy's heart began pumping. "So?"

He smiled. "Come on now, Ms. Uchello. The authorities were rather tight-lipped, said only that it had something to do with an investigation into illegal courier activity. Why don't you tell me your version."

"There is no version, only a few facts." Andy wondered if Victor was listening. Of course, he was. This was her chance to answer a few of his questions and perhaps salvage her job. "A man who calls himself Les Albright met me at DFW Thursday morning with the parcel I pick up for my regular trip to Seattle. He gave me the pouch I had paperwork for then offered to cut me in on another deal. He said he'd give me twenty-five hundred dollars if I would deliver a second package for him when I got to Seattle. I said no but he tricked me into being stuck with it." Her expression darkened just remembering all the trouble he had cost her. "When he contacted me the next day, I told him I didn't want any part of his deal, whatever it was, and that he'd have to come get the package I had put in the hotel vault for safekeeping. He came, I gave it to him."

"Aren't you leaving something out?"

"You mean the fact he was arrested?"

"That's what they tell me."

"Yes, I saw it happen." She bit her lip. "Look, I'm really sorry this happened while I was on company time. But I didn't do anything to encourage the man nor did I take a single penny from him. This job means too much to me to jeopardize it."

"Now, Ms. Uchello, are you telling me you had nothing to do with his arrest?"

Andy ducked her head, trying to keep cool but trying not to lie. She had told too many lies. "If you are asking me if I called the cops on him, then no. I never called anybody about the package."

"Why not? Wouldn't that have been the smart thing, the right thing to do if you were innocent of wrongdoing?"

Andy shrugged, wrapping the skirt of her robe more closely about her legs. She had felt guilty for so many reasons for so long, she wasn't certain she knew how innocent people behaved. "I didn't want to get involved."

"I see. But suppose you tell me why you didn't at least contact me so that I would know one of my people had been approached in this—suspicious manner?"

Andy smiled slightly. "I wanted to keep my job. I wasn't hurt, Zane Couriers wasn't compromised. I thought it best to keep silent."

"Is that what you plan to do, keep silent?"

"What else?"

"As I said, the federal authorities were tight-lipped. They did, however, mention the fact that your Mr. Albright named you in his deposition when he was arrested. He said you gave him the package, not the other way around. There are witnesses on the hotel staff to verify it."

Andy's jaw dropped. "That lying son-of-a—" She snapped her mouth shut. Of course Albright would say that. She expected he might. She just didn't know how quickly the word would spread. Victor had tried to tell her earlier. "So, what would you like me to do about it? Resign?"

Zane chuckled and sat back, stretching an arm along the sofa back. "Not at all. In fact, I'm thinking about rewarding you for your good behavior. Many a courier would have lost her head, run crying to the police or whatever. You handled it just fine, so far. Now, we just have to think about how to see to it that my business isn't dragged down by your little... indiscretion."

"My—" Andy stood up. "Look, Mr. Zane. I wasn't at all tempted by Albright's offer. If that's what you're thinking. He's a first-class sleaze with a come-on that wouldn't impress a junior high school student. I wouldn't risk my life and reputation for twenty-five hundred dollars."

"How about twenty-five thousand?"

Andy hoped again that Victor was listening. "I think you can go now."

"Now, now," Zane chided, still smiling and leaning back. "You can't be successful in a business like mine unless you know the people who are working for you. After Eric Connors disappeared last spring and the police discovered his name was an alias, I had a little detective work done myself.

"Eric was clever but not especially thorough. All he did was make it look as if there was a paper trail to back up his personal history. When my detective did a little digging your tissue of lies turned out to be as paper-thin as his, *Ms. Trask.*"

Andy accepted the stomach punch with no more than the tightening of her fingers on the green satin lapels at the neck of her robe.

"Daughter of Jake Trask," he went on with a sneer. "How's your daddy doing over there in Huntsville?"

Andy's chin shot up. "Don't know and don't care."

"I see. But, the adage certainly held true for you, didn't it? The fruit didn't fall very far from the tree. It was nice and convenient to learn you shared your daddy's history of a criminal record."

Though rage trembled through her, Andy held on to the idea that Victor already knew this, knew it before Albright was arrested. "So you know. Did you tell the authorities?"

Zane shook his head. "No need to open myself up to that. The appearance of reliability and tight security is all a courier service really has to offer its customers. I already had the liability of Eric Connors to deal with. If it became public knowledge that I had two ex-cons on the payroll, there'd soon be no business."

Eric was an ex-con. This bit of news shook her more than Zane's knowledge of her past. Yet, what he wasn't saying was more important than anything she had heard so far. "I don't believe you kept my secret just to protect your business."

Zane chuckled again, seeming to greatly enjoy himself at her expense. "You aren't shy. I like that in a woman. You're absolutely right. I don't want the police involved in my company. I can't afford to see where their kind of investigation would take them. Eric's trail led away from me. But if they began checking out all my employees, things could get, well, unpleasant."

A leap of insight widened her eyes. It answered the question that had bothered her from the moment Albright had shown up at DFW with her courier pouch. It was a shot in the dark but she had to take it. "Because Albright's on your payroll, too?"

His smile didn't leave his face but it congealed. "I wondered if you'd caught on. By his account, you were petrified to have that package in your possession."

"I've never been scared of anything or anyone." She paused to collect her ammo. "Not you, not Albright, not even my daddy."

"I see that. But you should know that a man like Albright doesn't respect courage."

"What does he respect?"

"It's just my opinion, of course, but I'd say it would have to be attached to money, big money, to interest him."

"Your money?"

Zane recoiled. "Now, I'm just a simple businessman. I don't know exactly what Albright's been up to and I want it to stay that way. I hired him to run my Chicago courier office. Pure and simple. If he's been dipping his oar in muddy waters he'll have to take the consequences." He smiled. "So, let's get down to brass tacks. I don't want you testifying in court about Albright or anything else. You got that?"

"And if I refuse, you'll trot out your information on my past and offer it to the police."

"I'd just be doing my duty as a citizen. How much time do you think you'll get for possession of illegal government documents? That is a nice passport you carry. Nobody's ever questioned its authenticity, have they, Ms. Trask?"

Andy felt a hard shiver go through her but her gaze never left his face. "Make it worth my while to keep silent."

He nodded in approval. "Now you're talking. But first you tell me what's made you decide after all these months to accept my hospitality?"

Andy shrugged. "I like money. Zane Couriers doesn't pay much and there are things I want."

He smiled. "You might have had a lot by just being nice to me before."

Andy let her anger show. "I don't do rich, older men for money. I have a few scruples."

He laughed. "You also have some mouth on you, Andy. I think I like it. But we've come a bit far to be coy now."

Andy concentrated on the fact that Victor was in the next room. Her answer was for him. "Meeting Albright was strictly an accident."

"I'd like to believe that. Why don't I believe it?"

"Because you can't afford to. Coincidences like that are too dangerous to accept. You wouldn't be able to sleep at night if you didn't believe that everything in your world revolves around you and you hold the strings that determine the height and speed of those orbits."

"A philosopher, too. Do go on, Ms. Trask."

But Andy merely shook her head. She had run out of bravado. She could only think about how she was going to lie convincingly through the next few minutes.

Zane nodded. "Fine. Then let's get back to business. The Feds can't force you to testify. They're accustomed to witnesses changing their minds. Fear of retribution, and all. So, what do you think happens after you show them—politely, mind you—the door?"

Andy glanced toward her bedroom before she could stop herself. To cover the blunder, she slowly crossed her legs, not stopping the slide of silk over silk. "I hope you're more creative than the average thug. A dead body leaves a stench that's hard to escape. Even for a man who wears hundred-dollar cologne."

"Now, now." He smiled approvingly as his gaze slid down her, lingering on the slim legs revealed where her robe had parted. "Since we've had our little chat, I'd hoped you have a better understanding of how I operate."

"Right." Andy kept a hammerlock on her nerves. She was perfectly safe. Victor was in the next room. Victor was a federal agent. He should be getting more than an earful. "If I say a word against Albright you'll tell the authorities who I am. While I'm marking time in prison for a crime like forgery of federal documents, who's going to listen to me?"

He grinned, looking like a man who'd just won the lottery. "You have a remarkably solid head on your shoulders, Ms. Trask. Maybe I could use your services, after all. Strictly in the business sense," he added as Andy let her enmity show. "Come on. You just said you want more than life has offered you so far. All you have to do is nothing and your life will continue as before, only better. What if I relocate you? You could be an overseas special messenger. You'll make big bucks, visit exotic places. Isn't that what you've always wanted?''

"Maybe." The air was thick with innuendo and she was no longer a stranger to intrigue. Once things calmed down, maybe in as little as a month from now, she could find herself in one of those wonderful exotic places alone. Then she just might come down with a fatal illness, or slip off a cliff. And no one would think to question it. No relatives to hassle the company for explanations. No one to mourn her loss. Like Eric, she would quickly become a sad but faint memory to her friends. All Zane needed was maybe a few weeks to solve his difficulties. She needed only five free minutes.

"I don't see that I even have a choice, do I? I'll take the assignment." Andy was once again on her feet. "I think you can find the door, Mr. Zane."

He rose slowly to his feet and glanced at her bedroom doorway. Andy felt her heart hit bottom. Had he seen a shadow, movement? His gaze swung back to her. "Sure you wouldn't like to entertain your boss a while longer? Maybe celebrate together?"

The proposition was so different from what she'd expected him to say, Andy smiled. "As I said before, I'm not interested in being anybody's paid companion."

"Why, Ms. Uchello, you wound me." His silver eyes glinted. "I don't buy women."

Andy let her natural antagonism cover for her wobbling knees. "With your reputation preceding you, how would you know?"

He laughed. "That's good." He tipped his hat to her before setting it on his head. "I'm going to enjoy working with you, Andy. You're like a straight shot of tequila after a diet of fruity cocktails."

He turned and opened the front door. She heard his exclamation of surprise as the top step rocked and then his foot slipped and his head or arm thumped the wall. "Watch out for the top step," she called belatedly, "it's loose."

The moment the door closed, she sprang across the room and shot the dead bolt home.

Applause sent her spinning round to find Victor standing just inside the room.

Andy gave him the thumbs-up sign as she crossed to him. "Did you hear that?" she whispered, in case Zane wasn't yet out of earshot.

"Every sweet word."

"You're dressed." Her tone was accusatory.

Victor grinned wickedly. "Sorry, *querida*. I've got business to take care of."

He pulled her in for a kiss. He meant it to be quick, a lover's apology for running out on such short notice. But something happened. He stayed to taste her and the tasting required a more thorough delving into the complicated mystery that she was. They were both breathing hard by the time they parted, leaning into one another for support.

He cupped her adorable face in both hands and pressed his forehead against hers. "I haven't thought so at any minute until now but your stepping into my case may be the best thing that's happened to it."

Andy had hooked her thumbs into the belt loops on either side of his waist. She tugged him closer. "What do you mean?"

Victor angled his upper body away from her so that he could see into her eyes. "Don't you get it? Albright's not the mastermind. Zane is!"

"Zane?" Andy made a face. "Get real. The Zane family helped coin the term 'Texas billionaire.' Why would Elijah Zane be in the least bit tempted by illegal money?"

Victor smiled in the face of her rank skepticism. "You're so naive. A regular Girl Scout." That brought out all her natural antagonism. Her face became a study in female indignation. He liked her best hot and spicy.

He laughed and gently wagged her head between his hands. "I can't tell you what draws some people into crime. For Zane it's probably the thrill, the challenge of getting away with it. There're very few things or people a man like Zane can't simply buy, one way or another. There's no sport in being the biggest gorilla in the room. Like most men, he probably craves the thrill of the hunt to get him up out of bed every morning."

"Does that include you?"

Victor smiled in self-knowledge. "Even me. I'm a lawman, Andy. I get to play some version of cops and robbers every day. Zane probably thinks of his illegal activities as a chess game. Maybe he gets his kicks by matching wits with the professionals."

"So that makes Albright, Eric and me pawns."

Victor nodded. "Something like that." He kissed her again, waltzing her back toward the front door, which he pressed her against so that their full lengths came into contact. "Damn! Sometimes, I hate this job," he muttered as he tore his mouth away from hers.

"The thrill of the hunt," Andy reminded him.

He parted her robe with his hands and reached for the warm willing woman beneath. "All the thrills I want are right here. Keep the home fires burning for your warrior, okay?"

He was halfway down the stairs before he remembered and turned back. "I left my car at the health club," he announced sheepishly when Andy opened the door. "Can you drop me off?"

Ten minutes later Andy was waving goodbye as Victor swung his car out of the club's parking lot. He was on his way to try to file for court orders to search Zane Couriers' Dallas and Chicago offices. He said he needed evidence linking Albright and Zane. That connection might be just the piece of evidence he needed to open Albright up and reel Zane in.

Andy sat drumming her fingers across the top of her steering wheel. She was too antsy to go home and wait around and too keyed up for the idea of food to hold any fascination. Her mind kept going back to Zane.

He had threatened her because, he said, he didn't want his name and his companies looked into by the authorities. If Albright was acting on his own, Zane might find the scrutiny embarrassing. But if, as Victor suspected, Zane was actually in charge he would—

"Need to destroy evidence!" she cried, surprising herself.

Andy turned the key in her ignition and floored the gas pedal. That's what Zane had been doing when he came to see her, buying time, not her silence. He needed time to cover up and destroy any connections between himself and Albright. He would probably toss her headfirst to the authorities once he had done that.

Andy murmured a curse. Zane believed his threat to expose her had made her too afraid to speak to the police on her own. Later, when they picked her up and then she began telling the truth, who would believe it was anything more than a fabrication of wild accusations she, a convicted felon, had pulled together to try to save her own neck? A rare smile of pleasure spread across Andy's face. Treasury Agent Victor Mondragon would believe her. That's who.

But even he had told her he needed proof. Victor was a by-the-book kind of guy. So then, she would get him proof, even if it was only a single thread. Dreams were sometimes held together by the slenderest of threads.

VICTOR ROARED into the corridor of their basement offices with a smile a foot wide. "We've got him, Phil! Wait till you hear where I've been."

"I don't have to ask," Phil said with a smirk as Victor brushed past him into his office. "When was the last time you looked in the mirror?"

Victor checked his step. "Why?"

Phil grinned. "I don't know, maybe it's just me, but I'd swear you should stay away from coral shades. They bring out the yellow undertones in your skin."

Victor swiped the left side of his mouth. Phil jerked his head to the right a couple of times. Victor tried again and this time a smear of Andy's lipstick came off on his hand. "Very funny."

Phil's face suddenly sobered. "Where the hell have—no, never mind. Why haven't you checked in?"

"I've been busy," Victor muttered as he rounded his desk and punched on his computer.

"That much I guessed. Things have been hopping since you disappeared..." Phil checked his watch "...five hours ago."

Victor looked up from his terminal. "It's not Albright, it's Zane! Elijah Zane, to be exact."

"Elijah Zane is what?"

"Our mastermind. He owns Zane Couriers and about a million other things. Banks, oil interest, cattle, financial networks worldwide. That kind of cash flow can float a lot of boats."

"So far the picture is as clear as mud."

"Sit down and I'll explain."

Phil shook his head. "Slow down, Vic. There's been a recent development in Seattle."

Something in his tone made Victor stop what he was doing and look up.

"Andre Erickson's dead."

"How?"

"You know we've been waiting since Friday for the FBI to clear it so we could go after him. The warrant didn't come in until this afternoon. Our agents say they couldn't have missed him by more than ten minutes. He drove his car off a cliff."

Victor smirked. "Where have I heard that before?"

"No. This time he was still inside with the seat belt fastened when the police arrived. Broke his neck."

Victor swore under his breath. "So, what was it, a hit?"

"Not according to witnesses. It happened in the middle of rush hour, 6:00 p.m. Witnesses say he'd been driving like a madman for miles. Finally, he swung out into oncoming traffic. Lost control, hit a guardrail, and rolled over the top. The rest would have made terrific Hollywood stunt footage, according to the local police.''

Victor swore again in Spanish. "Okay. We'll catch up on the back end of that one. Right now I need Chicago to give us everything they can grab in ten minutes on Albright's operation in Chicago, who pays the bills, who works there, any previous records, things like that. Most of all, I want any lead that we can trace back to a Zane corporation or holding.''

"What makes you think we've been after the wrong man?''

Victor smiled. "I heard the SOB boasting about it to Andy Uchello in her apartment not twenty minutes ago. Jesus! If only I'd had a tape recorder on me!''

"Entrapment?'' Phil suggested.

Victor grinned. "I was the only one cornered.'' He touched his face where the lipstick had been. "Push them in Chicago, Phil. I need a search warrant and I need it now!''

When Phil turned away, Victor reached for the phone. He hated telling Andy about Eric over the phone but he didn't want her to hear it from anybody else. She had been through so much. He hated that he wouldn't be there to hold her in his arms when she heard it. But, damn it, he could have used Eric's testimony against both Albright and Zane. Things were heating up. Fast.

The phone rang four times before he got her recorded message. "Andy, it's Vic. Call my office as soon as you get this. I'll be in late.''

After he hung up he stared at the phone a long time. Where could she be? They hadn't had dinner. Maybe she'd gone to get something before going home. He hoped she came back soon. He needed to hear her voice. He needed her pinned down. He knew she was perfectly safe yet instinct made him dial again.

He was furious by the time the answering machine picked up. "Don't do anything stupid, Andy!" he shouted and hung up.

ANDY SAT before her terminal entering combinations of flight arrangements, trying to find a pattern in the courier routes Eric had taken his last month on the job. Those records had been filed away but because she did data entry, she had access to all the regular files. She tried but was unable to get into finance. Ditto for contracts.

She had thought about calling Keisha, who had access to those files, but decided against it. Her supervisor had a family to think of. No need for her to stick her neck out tonight. But in the morning she would corner Keisha and make certain she understood that any help she could render in tracking down information against Zane would be looked upon favorably by the attorney general's office. At least, Andy supposed, that's who would take over the case.

She had been at it an hour when she suddenly saw a pattern leap out. The records said Eric had been flying the Chicago corridor exclusively in January yet she remembered him showing her three new visa stamps on his passport that month, one from the Bahamas, one to the British Virgin Islands and one to Grand Cayman.

Andy smiled as she hit the print button. She had kept his passport somewhere in the pile of his things. She'd have proof of something, even if she didn't know exactly what.

She scanned down quickly to February. Eric had told her he was scheduled to be in New York the night he died. There was no travel entry for that day. No tickets issued, either.

She moved back to December, trying to remember what their final Christmas together had been like. She had just begun flying the Seattle route. He had been rather jealous of her luck. Looking back on it, it was probably because he was doing Houston, New Orleans and Atlanta. Seattle was always overnight. His trips often weren't. Yet he had been absent a lot. Christmas had never been richer. He had bought her a full-length leather coat, two pairs of designer boots and a diamond bracelet. She'd had the bracelet only a few weeks before it disappeared. He scolded her for losing it but she suspected even then that he needed the money and had pawned it himself.

"Fool," Andy muttered as her eyes scanned the records. She had been so gullible.

Suddenly she was staring at records she had never seen. The month of December was filled with peg-ins, unscheduled flights that had to be filled in after the fact. There were five in all, four of them attached to Eric's name. Four trips to Mexico and one to Seattle. He had never said a word about any of them.

She punched the print button a second time.

The laser printer was remarkably quiet, still she didn't hear a sound until he was right behind her.

"Working late, Ms. Uchello?"

Andy leaped out of her chair, banging into the cubicle wall as she twisted around to face Elijah Zane.

The gun in his hand didn't surprise her as much as the fact he had gotten in without her hearing him. "What are you doing here?"

"Surprising a thief, or so I thought." He looked past her to her computer screen. "What are you doing here, Andy?"

"Catching up on old filing," she answered. A close look would make her a liar. "Is that just for effect or is it loaded?"

He looked surprised by her question but he didn't lower the barrel or aim it away from her. "I don't plan to do you any harm."

"I'm glad to hear that." Andy made herself look away from the gun. She even managed to reach for the monitor key and turn off the screen. "I'm sorry if my presence alarmed you," she said in a less than steady voice. "It's just that I've missed a lot of work lately. Friday, Monday and Tuesday, to be precise. I thought I'd come in and try to catch up. But I guess I should go home. It's—" She glanced at her empty left wrist. "Hmm, I must have left my watch at home."

"It's eleven-thirty," he supplied, watching her as intently as a cat might watch a moth.

"That late?" Andy said faintly. Inevitably, her gaze came back to the gun. It was silver and sleek, the bore small but deadly. She couldn't look away from it. "Don't you think it's time you put that away?"

She saw his fingers refit their grip. "Who sent you here? Connors?"

Andy's eyes lifted to his face. "What about Eric?"

He grinned. "You say you weren't working for Albright. But don't tell me this isn't a shakedown. If not Albright, then it's got to be Connors, or whatever the hell he's calling himself these days."

"It's true, I know Eric didn't die in that faked car crash last spring," she said to keep him guessing about her real intent. "But I didn't know where he was until last week."

"How did you find out?"

To her amazement she responded with the truth. "Albright told me. I saw Eric for the first time last Friday in Seattle. It was quite a conversation. He told me a lot of things."

"I knew it." The muscles in Zane's face bunched, distorting his handsomeness. "So, it was Connors. He always was a greedy little bastard. Wanted to live my life without putting forth the effort to get it." His gaze narrowed again as it rested speculatively on her. "I had begun to suspect he might be considering blackmail to get it. That's why I took action."

Andy noted that he had used a past tense verb twice in referring to Eric. Everything inside her went still but the pulsing of her heart. "What's happened to Eric?"

Zane shifted his gaze away from her for the first time. "I had him 'talked to.'" Annoyance flickered along his sharp cheekbones and cut a razor edge on his thin lips. "The boys must have scared the bejabbers out of him. He's dead." His expression altered, becoming focused again. "It was the call from Seattle that sent me down here to check on things."

Andy took a deep breath. "So, now you plan to have me 'talked to'?"

"No," he said without rancor. "Much as I regret it, I may just have to kill you."

"You won't get away with it," Andy heard herself say before she could stop the ridiculous cliché from popping out. "I mean, you were right to think I'm not acting alone. I'm working for the Treasury Department. Undercover."

She thought she would burst into hysterical laughter at the comical expression that crossed his face. For a few precious seconds, he actually believed her.

"Now, Ms. Trask," he said with a smile, "I expected more cleverness from a woman like you."

"I know," Andy answered remorsefully, wishing she had been more clever, like leaving a message in case Victor came looking for her. "But it's true. When you came to my place tonight, there was a federal agent there, hiding in my bedroom."

That did provoke laughter from him. "Now, I don't doubt any man worth the designation wouldn't jump at the chance to hide in your bedroom, Ms. Trask, but don't you think that tale's just a bit farfetched?"

It was outrageous. But it happened to be true. "I don't expect you to believe me but you will remember, won't you, when they come for you, that I told you the truth." Andy moved a little closer to the printer. "They already suspect you're behind the illegal courier ring. I was just trying to make things easier for them."

She glanced at the two sheets of paper lying in the printer rack. "You might as well let me go. The most I can do is talk. You can have me arrested for my crimes. But if you kill me, you'll have no less than a federal agent as a witness to testify to your earlier threats to me." Her gaze strayed again to the papers. "His name is Victor Mondragon, Mr. Zane. Remember it."

She saw him spare a gaze at the paper in the printer rack. "Hand me those papers, Ms. Trask."

Andy tensed. "Get them yourself."

The moment he moved toward her she knew she'd have only one chance. She backed up, blocking the printer. He waved her aside with the barrel of his gun. She waited until they almost touched before she slipped sideways away from him. She saw his free hand reach out for the papers and then she flung herself toward the open back of the cubicle.

"Hey!"

His shout almost buckled her knees but she didn't stop running. The cubicles were placed back-to-back down the middle of the long room with a long aisle on either side. He'd have a clear shot if he wanted it but she was betting, unwisely perhaps, that he wouldn't want to explain shooting a fleeing woman, an employee at that, in the back.

The thick carpeting all but muffled their rapid footsteps but not the roughened sounds of their labored breathing as they rushed like Olympians going for the gold toward the bank of elevators at the far side of the building.

The glass doors that separated the reception area from the main offices were usually locked. As Andy met them head-on she tried to remember if she had left them open. She lifted her hands palms-flat and plowed into them. The right side gave and she half stumbled through it, the stagger slowing her pace.

She felt Zane's hand drag at her hair but she twisted free, tears springing into her eyes. The elevator doors were closed. Was it on this floor or below? She glanced up at the numbers as she neared them. The one on the right was rising. She punched the Down button just as Zane caught up with her.

She had grown up hard and lived wild. She didn't fight nice. She punched and scratched and twisted and kicked and bit, completely surprising the man who was quite a bit taller and heavier than she was. She was winning until he gave up trying to be anything like a gentleman and landed a fist to her jaw.

Andy saw stars, big ugly bursts of distorted light that made spaghetti of her limbs and filled her mouth with blood.

"God damn you!" Zane roared. She dragged against the arm he put out to steady her as she slipped toward the floor. "I didn't want this. You forced me. You hold still now."

The chime of the elevator reaching their floor seemed to surprise both of them. A second later the copper doors parted and Victor Mondragon stood framed in the breach.

Andy saw that he was unprepared for the sight that confronted him. Yet, he was a veteran of unplanned events. She watched in helpless horror as he calculated the odds and then reached behind for his gun, saying, "Treasury Agent Victor Mondragon. Drop your weapon! You're under arrest!"

Beside her Zane fell back as his gun came up. He wasn't thinking, she realized wildly. Victor mustn't die because of her. Not that!

She pushed both feet against the floor and jammed the full force of her shoulder into Zane's middle as she rose from her half-crouched position. The force of her blow sent Zane barreling backward and she went with him.

She heard the deafening discharge of his weapon as they fell together and wondered why the explosion seemed to go off inside herself as well.

"No! No!"

Victor's voice faded rapidly, as if she were hurtling backward away from him and the room, and all reality of the last days. The peace was welcome. White oblivion.

Epilogue

The wind off the coast around Port Isabel was surprisingly mild for a late October day. The day was
overcast, the shallow gulf waters capped by foamy
waves that marked an offshore rainstorm. There was
just the pesky cry of gulls, the ceaseless sound of the
water, and the slim young woman walking alone at the
edge of the surf. She had pulled a bright orange Uni-
versity of Texas sweatshirt over her T-shirt and shorts.
That made it much easier for Victor to spot Andy as
he came up the beach from the parking lot.

He paused to watch her before she noticed he had
arrived. Eight weeks earlier he had stood in the emergency waiting room of Parkland Hospital in Dallas
and prayed that she would live to see another day.

He would never forget that moment when the elevator doors had parted and he'd seen her face, frightened and bloody but determined. He had come
because he'd known in his gut she was up to something. And for the first time since he'd met her, he'd
acted exactly as his instincts had suggested and
dropped everything in his office to come looking for
her. Only he hadn't expected to find her fighting for
her life.

She'd taken a bullet for him! Not caught a bullet meant for him, but tackled a man with a gun who was half again her size.

He had lived and died a lifetime as they fell together and the sounds of the discharging gun ricocheted off the walls.

The only good thing to come out of the moment was that she had frightened Zane into total surrender. He had thrown the gun away, crying, "You saw that! You saw her jump me! She made the gun go off. I didn't shoot her!"

Victor started jogging down the beach after her.

"Breathe, Andy! Breathe!" He had said the words over and over to her as he held her in his lap and covered Zane with his revolver while the businessman dialed 911. Longest fifteen minutes of his life. Longest night of his life, while she underwent surgery to remove a bullet from her shoulder where it had lodged after passing through her lung.

If she had died . . .

He shook his head, breathing in the salty air with relish, and wondered how other men knew they were loved. Andy had offered her life for his. It didn't get any more elemental or fundamental than that.

Strangely, that act had put a distance, a shyness between them that had carried over into her recuperation period. He had wanted her to stay with him, in his Dallas apartment, while she convalesced. Instead, she had chosen to move back to Cameron County with one of her former foster parents who had read about her heroic gesture and offered her a place to stay.

He had accepted that she needed time. But now it was time to find out what she really wanted. Maybe she'd been through so much that she didn't want any reminders of the hell she'd endured. Maybe she didn't want him. He had to know. He needed to know. Anything less than an outright rejection and he wouldn't go away easily or willingly. In fact, he wouldn't go away at all.

She finally heard him coming and paused in her strolling as he jogged up to her. She smiled at him but she didn't rush up to him so Victor thrust his hands into his pockets and smiled at her. "Hello, Andy."

"Hello, Victor." She didn't hold his gaze. As she turned to continue walking, he fell into step beside her. "How's the shoulder?"

"Almost as good as new." She patted the silky paisley scarf that formed her sling. "The doctor has me doing these strengthening exercises with a rubber ball. I'm going to have one heck of a handshake when I'm done."

"Does it still hurt?" Victor asked, not really wanting to talk about her arm but not quite knowing how to begin the conversation he wanted to have.

"Not much." She paused and bent to pick up a shell. "I should have come out here earlier today. Or maybe later, after the rain that's about to come ashore. It should drive lots of pretty shells up on the beach."

Victor reached out to curve a hand about her nape and draw her in. He was relieved when she stepped in close to him to lay her cheek against his jacket front.

"How was your flight?" she asked softly.

"I don't give a damn about the flight," he said roughly and wrapped his other arm carefully about her shoulders to hold her close. "I've been waiting two months to hold you, Andy. Just let me hold you. Okay?"

For once she didn't answer, just stood within his arms and let him press his cheek to her hair. She smelled, as always, of some elusive but markedly provocative perfume. After a moment he lifted her face to his. "My mother wants to thank the woman who could beat me to a bullet."

She smiled up at him. "Your mother is probably cordial to everyone who's nice to her handsome son."

"She's particularly partial to the woman who has gotten me to mention her name and the future in the same sentence."

Andy's gaze went blank. "We went over this before I left Dallas, Victor. You can't jeopardize your career. You don't know how Albright's trial will turn out. After that comes Zane's trial. You can't guess what the papers will make of my history. You can't imagine how awful it would be for you if it gets out to the tabloids that a Fed is dating an ex-con."

"As long as they get it right, that we're an item, I don't care about the rest."

"What about your mother?" She backed out of his arms and smiled, trying to make light of it all. "How would she like it if they made a TV movie about us? *The T-man and the Felon*. Has a certain tawdry quality, don't you think?"

Victor expelled a breath of exasperation. "Do you think I give a damn about what anyone else thinks? You took a bullet for me! I think that counts for something."

"It counts for stupidity!" Andy shot back, cradling the sling in which her injured arm rested. "I don't plan to make a habit of it, so tell your mother not to think too highly of me."

Victor smiled easily for the first time. Temper meant her emotions were engaged. That was better than whatever acting she'd been doing before. "You can tell my mother yourself. She's invited you to dinner next Sunday."

Andy cocked a brow at him. "If that's true, then tell her I genuinely thank her for the invitation but right now I'm a little low on cash. A trip to L.A., even to meet your mother, is out of the question."

"It's on me."

Andy shook her head. "Remember, I don't accept gifts I can't afford to pay back."

"You can pay me back. My mother has her heart set on this."

Andy sized him up with a look that made him shift from one foot to the other. "And what about her son?"

"You mean sons. I have three brothers and two sisters."

"Good grief. So many?"

"That's right and since I'm the only one not yet married you're going to have to deal with a lot of ribbing."

Andy shook her head, suddenly afraid. "I can't. I'm not good with crowds. I certainly don't know how to deal with big families."

"You'll learn."

"Maybe I don't want to learn." Her chin rounded in stubbornness. "Maybe I want to be left alone."

Victor's eyes narrowed. "What's wrong now?"

She hunched a shoulder and turned away. "Nothing."

"Andy?"

She began walking again and he followed to hear her say, "I talked to my lawyer today. He said the state is willing to cut a deal for me but there are no guarantees that they'll drop all the charges."

"They will."

She stopped and turned to him. "But—"

He put a finger to her lips. "Trust me."

She smiled behind his finger. "You know I do."

"Then believe it. You're going to walk away a free woman, until I can convince you to think about a stroll down a certain aisle."

Her dark eyes widened slightly but her tone remained contrary. "Don't rush me."

"Who's rushing?" He dragged his fingers along her lips, smiling as they parted softly to his teasing. "But you're coming to L.A. where I can keep an eye on you."

Andy licked the spot where his finger had passed. "Why L.A.?"

"Because I've been offered a desk job that rather appeals to me. I've been pretty busy these past years. I need time to kick back, collect a paycheck like other men and go home to my life every night. You know anybody who wants a roommate?"

"Maybe." Andy let her gaze drift from his gold eyes down to his mouth and wondered if he still tasted like sunshine. "If she can find a way to pay her share of the rent."

"You don't—" She touched his mouth.

"I want—" He wrapped his arms about her.

"Your choice."

"And don't forget it!"

He pulled her in until they were touching from chest to knees. "Andy?"

She leaned into him. "Hmm?"

"Are we ever going to just learn to be like every other couple?"

She smiled at him. "Oh, I hope not."

He grinned at her. "Something tells me it isn't even an option." He bent and kissed first one eye and then the other. "One more thing."

She opened her eyes, her lashes spiked by the passage of his tongue. "What?"

"My mother doesn't believe in this living together thing. Let me tell her that you're at least thinking about getting engaged but, for now, we have to be discreet. That way she'll know you respect me."

Andy lifted her good arm up to encircle his neck. "Victor?"

"Yes, *querida?*"

"*Besas me mucho!*"

"*Con mucho gusto, querida!*"

And he did until they were clinging to one another and smiling and dreaming of L.A. nights in the bed they had yet to buy.

HARLEQUIN®

I N T R I G U E®

**HARLEQUIN INTRIGUE AUTHOR KELSEY ROBERTS
SERVES UP A DOUBLE DOSE OF DANGER AND DESIRE
IN THE EXCITING NEW MINISERIES:**

THE ROSE TATTOO

In June we served up the first in "The Rose Tattoo" series,
#326 UNSPOKEN CONFESSIONS, which featured a tall, dark
and delectable hero and a sweet and sassy heroine.
Continuing on with the series, we're proud to present:

On the Menu for July - #330 UNLAWFULLY WEDDED

J. D. Porter—hot and spicy
Tory Conway—sinfully rich
Southern Fried Secrets—succulent and juicy

On the Menu for August - #334 UNDYING LAUGHTER

Wes Porter—subtly scrumptious
Destiny Talbott—tart and tangy
Mouth-Watering Mystery—deceptively delicious

Look for Harlequin Intrigue's response to your
hearty appetite for suspense: THE ROSE TATTOO,
where Southern specialties are served up
with a side order of suspense.

What if...

You'd agreed to marry a man you'd never met, in a town you'd never been, while surrounded by wedding guests you'd never seen before?

And what if...

You weren't sure you could trust the man to whom you'd given your hand?

Look for MAIL ORDER BRIDES—a romantic suspense duet by Cassie Miles.

Don't miss the second title:

> #332 THE SUSPECT GROOM
> Cassie Miles
> July 1995

MAIL ORDER BRIDES—where mail-order marriages lead distrustful newlyweds into the mystery and romance of a lifetime!

ANNOUNCING THE

PRIZE SURPRISE SWEEPSTAKES!

This month's prize:

L-A-R-G-E—SCREEN PANASONIC TV!

This month, as a special surprise, we're giving away a fabulous FREE TV!

Imagine how delighted you and your family will be to own this brand-new 31" Panasonic** television! It comes with all the latest high-tech features, like a SuperFlat picture tube for a clear, crisp picture...unified remote control...closed-caption decoder...clock and sleep timer, and much more!

The facing page contains two Entry Coupons (as does every book you received this shipment). Complete and return *all* the entry coupons; **the more times you enter, the better your chances of winning the TV!**

Then keep your fingers crossed, because you'll find out by July 15, 1995 if you're the winner!

Remember: The more times you enter, the better your chances of winning!*

PTV KAL